Mr. Singh
AMONG
THE
Fugitives

a novel

Prepared for the press by Katia Grubisic
Cover design by Debbie Geltner
Book design by WildElement.ca

Library and Archives Canada Cataloguing in Publication

Henighan, Stephen, 1960-, author
    Mr. Singh among the fugitives / Stephen Henighan.

Issued in print and electronic formats.

ISBN 978-1-988130-29-3 (paperback).—ISBN 978-1-988130-30-9 (epub).—ISBN 978-1-988130-31-6 (mobi).—ISBN 978-1-988130-32-3 (pdf)
    I. Title.
PS8565.E5818M7 2017   C813'.54   C2016-907017-4
                                                C2016-907018-2

Printed and bound in Canada.

The publisher gratefully acknowledges the support of the Government of Canada through the Canada Council for the Arts and the Canada Book Fund, and of the Government of Quebec through the Société de développement des entreprises culturelles.

Linda Leith Publishing
Montreal
www.lindaleith.com

Mr. Singh AMONG THE Fugitives

a novel

STEPHEN HENIGHAN

ONE
a plain tale from the hills

To be a fifth son, even in a family of means, is to know that you must make your own way. My father told me that I would have a handsome send-off. After that, I would become what I made of myself. He longed for me to enter the world of commerce and, though I feared disappointing him, I knew from boyhood that I was not made to run my life in pursuit of values that spiral and plummet. By inclination, I am a squire: a man of leisure, property, and learning.

At the Academy, where I followed my elder brothers to school, the presumption of superiority soaked into my skin, just as a cultivated English, more Oxford than Bombay, drenched my vocal chords. The masters despaired of me: was I really the sibling of those assiduous young men who were distinguishing themselves in our emerging market? I read too much yet studied too little. I was interested in cricket only as a spectator. The games master never tired of reminding me that my eldest brother had been a left-armed fast bowler, the second had hit for six on his first appearance in the school colours, the third ... No, that was not me. To rush back and forth across the cricket pitch was preparation for a life consumed by undignified haste. I dreamed of a village of picturesque antiquity where I could be recognized as a man of culture; time for my books; a sinecure that would free me from running after money; and the company of sophisticated women. My final wish surprised my schoolmates, who had taken my indolence as evidence of sexual inversion. The day I was caned for reading magazines that had pictures of girls, the other boys indulged me as an exemplary slave of sanctioned lusts. Out of term, they began to invite me to parties.

Being picturesque made me popular. I remembered this lesson.

A lesson, though learned, cannot always be applied. One must find oneself in propitious circumstances. Where, in the teeming confinement of India, was I to locate my idyll? At university I read English literature.

"English loiterature," my eldest brother, already a towering business wallah, murmured. "You should be making your way in the world."

To annoy him, I loitered longer, remaining at university for a Master's degree. For three years I pretended to be writing a thesis on Rudyard Kipling. *Kim* and *Plain Tales from the Hills* satisfied my thirst for anachronism. Yet satisfaction, I discovered, is no motor for prose: after three years, when all I could show my supervisor was a perfunctory introduction, he suggested that I spare us both embarrassment by withdrawing from my degree. Generations of Indians, he reminded me, had included such qualifications on their curricula vitae: *M.A. Bombay (failed)*. I had written myself into an ancient tradition.

But where would I live my life?

Not beneath the critical eyes of my brothers. I dreamed of London—the London of Charles Dickens and Sherlock Holmes, of fog and gas lamps, where street Arabs sang ditties and sleuths pursued miscreants. I trembled to imagine London today. Knowing I would not endure a reality that sullied my most cherished literary memories, I preserved London as the territory of my imagination. I sought a blank space where I could dream myself into a new life. After thwarted plans and false starts, I emigrated to Canada.

My B.A. and M.A.—I suppressed the treacherous *failed*—were evaluated as equivalent to the training received at a Canadian secondary school. This was my first taste of Canadian naivety. In fact, it was my secondary-school training that was equivalent to their M.A.! But, as I wished Canada to indulge me, I indulged Canada. I cut a stately figure: the underdeveloped immigrant pleading to be admitted to modernity. I supplicated for a student visa to study English literature. I even offered to populate the Canadian wilderness by applying to a new university in the bush. Lakehead University. The name smacked of *mens sana in corpore sano*.

Absconding like a fugitive, I boarded a plane to a spot far beyond my brothers' scrutiny.

TWO
a passage to india

I arrived in Thunder Bay in September. The weather was clear and devoid of thunder; the chill lacerated my bones. The man sent from the university to fetch me from the tiny airport told me that the rocky headland that prodded into the bay was believed to be a sleeping Indian. I stared at this mass of bald stone. It did not look the least bit like an Indian. I marvelled at Canadians' misapprehensions. I shuddered at the cold. The temperature was fifteen degrees centigrade! "So this is the Canadian winter," I said. "It certainly is chilly."

"You ain't seen nothing," the driver said. "Wait until January when it's thirty-five below."

"Surely," I said, uncertain what he meant by *below*, "it cannot get colder than this?"

When lessons began, I saw that the other students were eighteen years old; the literature class was intended for children of twelve. The town of Thunder Bay, while it resembled a village, lacked the antiquity I sought. It was not an English village. It did not have thatched Tudor cottages or an undulating village green. No retired colonels who had served in the Punjab walked spunky terriers through the morning mist. In spite of the lake, almost as vast as an ocean, on whose shores the sleeping Indian reposed, mist was rare in Thunder Bay. It was a climate of harsh extremes. I was despondent at the thought that life in an English village was not my destiny. Should I have moved to England, after all? Had I betrayed my dreams by coming to Thunder Bay? I resigned myself to staying here, though I feared that I would always regard Canada as second best. In this I followed the example that Canadians set for me. My fellow students admired grandparents who had retired to Florida, parents who shopped in Chicago and New York, or actors who, though they appeared on American television speaking in American accents, were known to have been born in Canada. The deprecation of one's choice of nation, I grasped, was a Canadian habit.

In spite of the Canadian students' predispositions to self-abasement, I was unable to lord it over them. In Thunder Bay, high prices kept me poor; the cultural offerings could make one think only of Mahatma Gandhi's observation that Western civilization would be a very good idea.

As it was clear that none of my first three conditions for a good life—a beautiful village, a cultured life, financial security—could be met here, I concentrated on the fourth. In class, one of my professors mentioned that the current Prime Minister of Canada, when he was Minister of Justice, had decreed that the state had no place in the bedrooms of the nation. My ears pricked up at these words. I scanned the classroom, casting an expectant look at my female classmates. I realized too late that my bearded young professor was doing the same. The response he elicited was far more enthusiastic than any that I obtained. Two young women remained after class to talk with him. I lingered until it was clear that they were ignoring me.

In Canada, I observed, young women became amusing mainly after consuming large volumes of alcohol. When I approached girls who did not drink, they told me they were Christians: alcohol, alas, was not the only lapse from which they abstained. Their doctrinal rigidity sent me back to the girls who drank. I doubted that my slender body would withstand the gallons of beer that the tall boys from the university's hockey and football teams consumed—or, as they said, *chugged*. I knew that, rather than competing with them, it was incumbent upon me to offer something different. For a few weeks I tried to look like a brown-skinned hippie. Like some other male students, I grew my hair. I ceased to shave. The results were not those I had anticipated. One girl asked me if I was a guru. A youth with vacant eyes wanted to know what "karma" meant and whether a procedure known as "LSD" enabled one to glimpse the infinite. Attracting such company made me regret my decision to grow my hair. The attention of women was no closer; the company of fools, on the other hand, had become unavoidable.

Disconsolate, I felt like a caricature of myself. I worried that I could not be other than a caricature when I was the only Indian in Thunder Bay. But I had decided to uproot myself; I must accept the consequences. On a day when I did not have lessons, I went in search of a barber. I bowed my head against the cold. My brothers, for all their brawn, would not have believed that a man—particularly an Indian man—could walk through the icy blast of twenty degrees below zero without perishing. I had a woollen hat (I had learned to call it a *toque*) pulled down over my ears and a scratchy scarf drawn up over my mouth. My bulky parka weighed on my shoulders. Walking with my head lowered, I got lost. I found myself in a district of my town where I had not set foot before. I did not find a barber, but, to my astonishment, I saw a sign that read *Singh's Quick Curries*.

I was not the only Indian in Thunder Bay! I was not even the only Singh. Here were people who shared my name and nationality. As I opened the steamed-up glass door, a gust of hot korma tantalized my nostrils. A burly Sikh about forty years old looked up from behind a counter where he was ladling basmati into a Styrofoam takeaway container. In a Punjabi that I was able to decipher, he asked: "Why have you come here?"

My compatriot served his customer, rang up the purchase at the till, then looked at me again as though I were an apparition. I wondered whether he did not have a point. Why had I come to Canada? To Thunder Bay?

I remained silent.

It didn't matter. S. A. Singh, sole owner and proprietor of Singh's Quick Curries, introduced himself in a burst of jovial greeting. Of course his name was Singh; all Sikh men used this surname. For them it was a way of erasing the false social distinctions of the caste system. For me it was simply a common surname that might belong equally to a Sikh or a Hindu.

"We are brothers!" S. A. said with a laugh. He welcomed me as a lost soul, a wandering foreign student who was too far from home to know how to look after himself. A married man with two children and his own business, he seemed to feel an obligation to take me under his wing. He served me chicken korma and, leaving his adolescent daughter, a girl in a Toronto Maple Leafs sweater, behind the counter, sat down with me at one of his takeaway's three tables.

"You look like a vagabond or a fugitive," S. A. said, once we had exchanged desultory information about our families. He interrupted our conversation to shout instructions at his daughter, Seema. He spoke in Punjabi and I in Hindi. Once I had finished my korma—there was no question of his charging me for it—he switched to English, and our roles changed. His English was loud, with a strong Canadian twang. "You sound like a Brit," he said. "And you look like a deviant. We've got to do something about that hair."

"I was on my way to the barber."

"In my family, you don't go to the barber, you learn how to tie a turban."

"That is hardly appropriate for a Hindu."

He laughed. "Canadians can't tell the difference between Hindus and Sikhs. They don't even know where India is. Half the people who come in here think I'm some sort of Arab!"

I stared at this strange man, feeling that I had taken passage to India—to the India that existed outside India: an India-in-a-nutshell that endured among confused emigrants scattered to the farthest reaches of the known world.

I sipped the tea that S. A.'s daughter brought us. "I don't know how to tie a turban," I murmured.

"I'll show you." He stood up. I felt a squeeze of alarm. Did this madman imagine he was making a religious convert? His smile, though, was reassuringly sardonic. "It's always good to know how to put on a turban." As his laughter died away, he said: "Then you may go on your way and visit the barber."

11

I felt soothed, though my head remained top-sy-turvy. My culture had acquired a lightness that made me dizzy. Two months earlier I had been in India, where culture is not a word but flesh and being, where religion is not a costume but a man's essence. I did not think that S. A. Singh was a bad man, but rather that he had drunk the waters of Canadianness more deeply than I would be comfortable doing. Our madcap midday party continued. I told myself not to be troubled because this was not serious; yet this lack of seriousness was what troubled me.

He disappeared into the back of the shop. Seema served chicken curry to two youths, bantering with them in a way that was inappropriate for an Indian girl. They talked about hockey. "If you're down at the arena on Friday night," one boy said, "I'll buy you a beer."

"You better not be bullshittin' me," Seema said. "If I go down there, I expect my beer."

She fell silent as her father returned, yet the spectacle had disoriented me. She looked like an Indian girl but spoke like someone else. An Indian girl did not drink beer or consort with boys. Was recklessness a family trait? This riddle twirled in my mind as her father spread his arms wide to display a vast piece of bright blue cloth. I had taken turbans for granted without knowing much about them. It had not occurred to me that the fabric Sikhs used was longer and wider than the fitted sheet on a king-sized bed.

"First," S. A. said, "you must put on a turban cap." He passed me a tight-fitting white cap. I struggled to push my bedraggled locks onto the top of my head, then pulled down the cap over them. The girl smiled at me as though we were fellow sufferers of her irrepressible papa. Had I ever visited an Indian family where a young woman had smiled at me in such a brazen way— and, to top it off, with her father standing there? I silenced the derogatory epithets that rose into my mind, the remarks I would have made had I discussed this incident with my classmates at the Academy. I knew that this girl was depraved, yet I recognized, also, that by coming to Canada I had lost the privilege of condemning her depravity. By the same token, she had gained the privileges of drinking beer at fifteen and smiling at a strange man who was being subjected to her father's caprices.

S. A. stood me up in the middle of the shop, amid the burble of boiling water and the shuffle of cutlery on the counter as his daughter served curry. "You fold the sheet like this, then you fold it again. You start like this," —his big hairy hands held my head in place, "—with a tail of fabric down the back. Then you wind it around and wind it again."

In truth, this turban business was not so difficult. Like all revered customs, it was a sequence of gestures. The realization perturbed me. It lingered, as I knew the image of Seema consorting with Canadian boys would linger in my mind.

When S. A. had finished securing the final fold of this curious weight on my skull, he smiled. I felt not ridiculed, but dignified. S. A. led me to a small, grubby toilet where I was able to look in the mirror. What a fine, self-confident fellow smiled back at me! I no longer looked like a deviant, or a bedraggled hippie. I was a man of substance, yet also, in Canadian eyes, I suspected, of mystery. If I wore this accoutrement to class, the girls in my lessons would wonder what wisdom I had trussed up in my brilliant blue cloth. The turban even enhanced my physical presence. I looked taller.

"Do you like it?" S. A. asked.

"I like it a lot." I glanced at him. "I would like to take it with me. I will pay you for it, of course.

It is a huge piece of fabric."

"It was a just a joke, my friend." He shrugged his shoulders. "A lark. I wasn't trying to convert you." Now his smile was nervous. Did he fear that he had stumbled on a fellow who was more deranged than he was?

"I want to buy the turban," I repeated. I could sense Seema, on the other side of the room, staring at me. "I will pay you a fair price."

"All right, my friend," S. A. said in a quiet voice. "If that is what you want." He shuffled his feet. His smile returned. "This is all in good fun, right, brother? It is my way of welcoming you to Thunder Bay. My way of inviting you to come back and visit us again."

THREE
under western eyes

I walked back through the snow to my dormitory, not barbered as I had planned, but carrying an enormous piece of blue fabric and a white turban cap in a plastic bag. How fortuitous that my surname happened to be the same as that used by Sikhs! Was it a sign, an indication of the path I should take in Canada? I imagined myself wearing my bright blue turban as confidently as Seema wore her navy blue Toronto Maple Leafs sweater. Her garment was a declaration of Canadian belonging; my destiny, paradoxical as ever, was to forge belonging by establishing myself as separate and apart. But the thought of masquerading as a Sikh, even for an evening at a party, in the hope of eliciting female attention, made me pause. As I paused, I felt my heart sicken. A man of Victorian inclination, I had come to the West because I felt Western. Even if marking myself off as Eastern and foreign stimulated Western curiosity, and especially female curiosity, I was reluctant to participate in the charade. A Sikh! What would my father say? He had brought me up to see Sikhism as a reforming strain in the great tradition of Hinduism. Sikhs, he had stressed, were not really different from us, they had merely chosen to exile themselves to a kind of borderland.

These memories swarmed over me as I closed the door of my miniature dormitory room, more like a space capsule than a living area, and dropped the plastic bag on the bed. I thought of S. A.'s warmth and hospitality. He did not seem to care that we came from different religious backgrounds, only that we were both Indians in the frozen north. And if the Sikhs lived in a borderland, so did I, with an education more English than Asian, a present in which I was learning about hockey rather than cricket. Against my will, I was gripped by the thought that the intermediate zone of Sikhdom might match my present state better than any declaration of purity.

I sat down to think about this.

I considered wearing my turban to the party in the lounge of my dormitory that Saturday night. In the end, I slid the plastic bag under the bed. I gathered my hair into a ponytail, went downstairs, and peered in the door, where titanic quantities of beer were being chugged. Enormous hockey players—in my eyes, all white Canadian men were hockey players—stumbled around the lounge as though they had ventured onto the ice without their skates. It was not the place for a hippie, or an Indian, or anyone who was not six feet tall. As I trailed back to my dormitory room in loneliness, I told myself that I must find my way, my means of asserting myself. I decided to lay Sikhdom aside and polish my reputation as a man of culture. If I could not chug beer, I would find an alternative. I settled on wine. I would present myself as a connoisseur of wine. I had never tasted wine. But, where I knew I would make a fool of myself if I tried to match the hockey players' slaking of beer, wine was linked to culture. It was part of the world I wanted. I was confident that there were young women who also yearned for this sophistication. I borrowed books on viticulture from the university library—the scant reading for my courses did not detain me for long—

and soon became knowledgeable. Knowledge, alas, is not visible. I felt ashamed at having to learn this lesson again. In truth, I'd known it already: I had arrived in Thunder Bay possessed of far more reading than my fellow undergraduates—was I not *B.A. Bombay, M.A. Bombay (failed)*?—yet neither my classmates nor my professors gave me credit for this learning. I needed to announce my difference. I needed an identity which, as my history professor said of the identity of the French province of Quebec, was *distinct*.

I sat down on my bed, reached beneath it, and pulled out the plastic bag. I stood before the small mirror on the wall and concentrated on replicating the movements S. A. had shown me. They weren't difficult to recall: as I had told myself, they were simply a series of gestures. Within ten minutes, my turban crowned my head. I looked like an illustrious fellow. I paraded back and forth across my room until walking that way felt natural. On Sunday night I again practised being a Sikh. On Monday I wore my turban to my lessons. Professors who had ignored me now treated me with cautious deference. My classmates stared. Many of these stares—particularly female stares—were stoked by curiosity.

In the halls after class, in the cafeteria, and in the corridors of my dormitory, I received questions not only from the blank-eyed oddballs who had asked me if I was a guru and knew how to glimpse the infinite, but also from young women who liked to read, were majoring in English or History, and were interested in foreign countries and cultures. My turban did for me in Thunder Bay what the magazine with photographs of girls had done for me at the Academy: it made me normal. As the only brown-skinned person in a class of straw-haired pale-faces, I was abnormal; my turban acknowledged the abnormality, smoothing the way for strangers to approach me. It opened the door between me and them, making it easier for everyone to speak with me. With girls whom I liked, I edged the conversation away from meditation or transcendence to the subject of wine. As I did so, I felt the young women relax. I was exotic but not too exotic: like other men, I offered the opportunity to drink and cavort. I merely did so in a way that was steeped in culture. As we bantered, I discovered that my initials, R. U., flowed easily from Canadian lips.

My dormitory room was as bleak as any other, but it was never lacking in bottles, or candles. A bottle of wine on a table, the lights turned off and the candle sputtering, conversation, invariably naive, about art and antiquity: all this rarely failed to produce the desired result. By the end of Lakehead University's fall semester, I was a man of the world. My trysts might have been with veritable untouchables, but they were untouchables with white skin, firm thighs, and perfect breasts. Across two continents and an ocean, I felt my brothers burn with envy.

north and south

Tuition fees, residence fees, the foreign student levy, wine, and the exorbitant cost of groceries and a winter coat depleted my handsome send-off. By December, I faced the prospect of spending the Christmas holidays alone in my dormitory with a handful of Chinese students and threadbare finances. When an envelope arrived containing a card decorated with a painting of a wilderness landscape, and, on the back, a scribbled invitation to Christmas dinner, I was exultant, even though I could barely decipher the handwriting. The invitation ended, "Most sincerely, Sam." Who was Sam? After reading the card a second time, I realized that my would-be host was S. A.

It had not occurred to me that Christmas was

celebrated in Canada, far less by Indians. Christmas! The very word evoked Merry Old England. I thought of Mr. Pickwick on his way to Dingley Dell. But what could Christmas mean among bare rock, withered pine trees, and frigid gales moaning off an endless lake? Nothing felt so far removed from England's green and pleasant land. Of course this was another of S. A.'s larks, as showing me how to tie a turban had been. Yet, as that incident had proved, toying with the boundaries between cultures could have long-term consequences. My Hinduism had always been passive rather than active, agnostic rather than fervent. Though a man of Victorian inclinations, I saw little point in agonizing over a crisis of faith. Now I wore a turban. Did a man in a turban lose his Far Eastern credibility if he celebrated Mr. Pickwick's favourite holiday? I'd have expected him to celebrate Diwali, in a strained, artificial way, humouring the children by dressing it up as a substitute for Christmas. Yet I understood his urge to dispense with such charades. We were in Canada, where, apparently, Christmas was as ingrained as it was in the land of Dickens. It made sense to plunge into the local waters.

On December 25, after tying my turban with

precision, I walked through streets so empty that the waves of snow seemed to have extinguished humanity. The glass door of Singh's Quick Curries was bolted shut. I went around to a side door. Seema, dressed in a merry red Christmas sweater that was pulled tight over her exuberant bosom, greeted me with a smile. Recognizing in her a knowing look purged of innocence, which I relished when, by candlelight, white Canadian women turned it in my direction, I responded with warmth. I then realized what I was doing and felt appalled. This was precisely how I had been taught not to look at an Indian girl. Nor should I expect an Indian girl to look back at me in such a way. When she opened her mouth, her brazen speech reminded me that she was not Indian. Her father hurried up behind her. His bellowed greeting trailed away at the sight of my turban. "Why are you wearing that piece of tomfoolery? This was a joke between us."

Seema retreated.

"Why are you signing yourself Sam?" I countered. "That's not your name."

Hostility jostled between us. I had not expected this. I had imagined myself greeted by the S. A. who loved a good joke, not by this censorious fellow.

I stood on the doorstep, the blood-sapping cold at my back. Toeing a rubber mat inside the door while the sounds of Christmas carols tinkled over his shoulder, S. A. replied, "I am Canadian now. As you will be if you stay here. I recommend the taking out of Canadian citizenship. It makes a man feel like he belongs."

"If you're Canadian," I replied, beginning to get angry, "why are you wearing a turban?"

"I am Canadian and Sikh. You are neither. You're making a damn fool of yourself." Refusing to budge from the doorway, he lowered his voice. "Do you think I invited you here simply to sing 'Jingle Bells'? I am concerned about my daughter. She is fraternizing with Canadian boys. I need to find her an Indian husband. I thought that a university-educated fellow like yourself, from a respectable family—"

"But I am not Sikh."

"We are not in Amritsar. We are not even in Bombay or New Delhi. We are in Thunder Bay, Ontario, Canada. I will settle for an Indian man— any Indian man, as long as he is a decent man. But you come here dressed like a harlequin. How can I take you seriously? My wife will think that you are mocking us. My daughter will giggle at you and go back to her hockey players." Running out of breath, he regarded me with a sigh to which the frigid temperatures lent an asthmatic wheeze.

"Please take off your turban."

"Let me come in."

"Come in and take off your turban."

I crossed the threshold of his family's rooms off the back of the shop. Without presenting me to his wife or son, he hustled me through a kitchen-dining room of linoleum and yellow wallpaper spotted with brown stains. Seema watched me subordinate myself to her father. I was resentful at having fallen in her estimation; the visit was ruined. I had not come here to flirt with her, yet as soon as S. A.—Sam?—had broached the possibility, the thought that I might supplant hockey players had become tantalizing. I did not compete with hockey players for the girls who came to my dorm room: my trysts were with young women who sought someone more cultured than a defenceman. To wrest Seema away from the husky fellows down at the rink would be a triumph. Or it would have been. My turban had ruined my chances. This was evident from the irate haste with which S. A. tore the garment from my head and tossed it onto the bed he shared with his wife.

"Let us see what we can do with that mop of yours."

He twisted my hair into a bun, which he lodged on the back of my skull. When I glanced in the mirror, I looked like a housewife, or a preadolescent Sikh boy who did not yet wear a turban. I resembled S. A.'s young son, the baby brother of my would-be betrothed. Over Christmas lunch, Seema refused to look at me. I reciprocated her disregard. I was polite to S. A.'s wife; I asked his son about hockey. S. A. was in a bad mood, and so was I. We listened to Christmas carols on the radio, but made no effort to sing along as we ate our curried turkey.

Having expected to stay into the evening, I left at three o'clock. S. A. accompanied me to the door. "In February," he told me, "when business is slow and airfares to India are more reasonable, I will close the shop for six weeks, remove my children from school, and take my family to the Punjab. There I will find a suitable husband for Seema."

He uttered the words as though they were an insult. Freeing myself from the ridiculous bun he had given me, I said: "I want my turban back."

He frowned at me. "You are not a Sikh. Why

27

do you wear a Sikh turban?"

"It is not a Sikh turban," I replied. "It is *my* turban."

I had not imagined this answer until it sprang from my mouth. Once I had uttered these words, I felt that my place in Canada had become clear to me.

I waited on the doorstep for S. A. to bring me my turban. I walked back to the university and spent the rest of the holidays alone in my dormitory. When lessons resumed after the long, vacant winter holiday, I was in a fix. I had failed French, Political Science and Canadian History; my two English literature classes had been elementary, yet my sonorous essays had left my professors unmoved. They reprimanded me for not interrogating literature from my position as a *visible minority*. They asked how I could remain *complicit* with the discourses of *patriarchy* and *heteronormativity*. They described my essays as Victorian. I received this as a compliment until I understood that it was a justification for giving me a mark of C.

During the bleak Christmas holiday when, as my driver had promised, the temperature dropped to thirty-five degrees below zero, a letter from the registrar's office had informed me that I was on academic probation. During the first week of January, I was summoned to see a counsellor, who told me that in order to maintain my status as a full-time student, I must be disciplined, I must work hard, I must *struggle*.

I do not struggle: such indignity is beneath a Victorian gentleman. Adding a line to my curriculum vitae—*B.A. Bombay, M.A. Bombay (failed), B.A. Lakehead (failed)*—I left. I did not even go to Singh's Quick Curries to say goodbye. The Chinese students had told me that in Toronto winter temperatures were milder. One of my paramours—was it Shelley or Melissa?—had asked me why I didn't choose to study in a place that was more *multicultural*. I had not heard this word before. She gave me to understand that it meant there were many Indians. I had a cousin in Toronto. Everyone on the planet, I would learn, has a cousin in Toronto. Mine was more accommodating than most. When I told him I would be arriving on the Greyhound bus, he agreed to take me in.

Whether it was the right or the wrong decision to slip away from the wilderness like a fugitive, I cannot say. My cousin, having been in Canada for many years, knew people who helped me parlay my student visa into a permanent resident's permit. Yet I lost my sense of myself, and would not regain it for many years. As some men speak of their years at war, so I recall my years in Toronto: a grim, grey time when I kept my head down and survived the shrapnel. I lived in drab apartments in towers long bus rides from final subway stops, which in turn were a lengthy journey from the city centre. No one cared about, or respected, my education or my reading. My cousin was outraged when I appeared with a beard and a Sikh turban. "You make a mockery of us all! We must show these Canadians that we have an authentic culture. They have no culture!" I preserved my new dignity until a pair of spotty-faced dacoits thrust me up against a cement wall near the subway station, pummelled me, and tried to tear my turban from my head.

After that, I went about short-haired and clean-shaven. Without my turban, I was nobody. In the summer months, I wore a Toronto Maple Leafs baseball cap. No garment had ever felt so empty; my baseball cap drained intelligence from my brain. I read Anthony Trollope and Elizabeth Gaskell on the subway, but had no one with whom to discuss their art. The buildings where I lived, and those where I worked, were grimier enlargements of my dormitory in Thunder Bay. I was a pizza delivery man, a distributor of flyers to automobile windshields, a stocker of shelves in a large grocery, a loader and unloader of cartons in the warehouse of a big-box store, an assistant to an installer of refrigerators in cheap apartments. Like Kipling's Kim, I drummed my heels on the pavement. I saw filthy corridors and three-bedroom flats crammed with a dozen beds, inhaled the odours of the unwashed, spent my days alongside tattooed men who spoke in curses, until I sympathized with the decision of my cousin and his friends to live only among our *community*.

"Community" was not a word I would have used prior to my arrival in that grey, slushy city where, as the Chinese students had promised, the temperature rarely sank to thirty-five below. In Toronto, "community" meant people who looked like you. Here the air was never as clear as in Thunder Bay. Blended cloud and smog seeped into one's brain. I felt that I was neither in Canada nor in India. I kept my head lowered. I enjoyed the vindaloos and biryanis that bubbled in cauldrons when my cousin and our flatmates and their cousins and their cousins' wives and children gathered on weekends. Yet I despaired of their disconnection: their ignorance of Canadian life, on which I informed myself by reading the newspapers; their mistrust of anyone who was not Hindu; the withdrawal of their bewildered children from school each February, when airfares to India dropped and everyone went "home" for one or two months.

Each time such expeditions were organized, I wondered who Seema had married.

My cousin and his friends asserted this supposed community as the core of our beings when the core of our beings was earning Canadian dollars. I pitied the rudderless young men, forbidden to hold uninhibited Canadian girls in their arms, who were told that they must marry an Indian virgin whom their parents would recruit from "home." I held myself apart from this dance, resisting all attempts to marry me off to supposedly suitable girls, who had been born in Toronto but were more assertively, provincially Indian than any girl from India. I resisted and resisted until my cousin asked me whether I liked girls at all. If only he knew! If only he had seen Melissa or Shelley. Refusing to answer his impertinent questions, I withdrew into myself.

I did not want to talk about my conquests,

not only because my cousin would be shocked, but also because the worst part of my life was that, in the tower-block ghettos a raucous bus ride from the end of the subway line, I no longer drank wine with Canadian girls. I rarely saw a Canadian girl. There were Somalis and Jamaicans and Chinese and Russians and Sri Lankans and Filipinos and Indians and Pakistanis. On crowded buses, they all acted like ruffians. The few Canadians who lived in our districts were more likely to call me a Paki than to think me picturesque. Toronto perpetrated a monstrous hoax against me: having adopted picturesque garb in order to be embraced by Canadians, I had been sewn into my native costume, trapped in a permanent game of charades, defined by my "community," even after I replaced my turban with a baseball cap. I despaired of being able to weave myself into Canadian reality as I had done in the dormitory in Thunder Bay. I knew, of course, that in the Victorian houses downtown and in certain posh districts north of downtown there were well-off Indian families who sent their children to Canadian universities, where they studied with Canadians, worked alongside well-off Canadians and sometimes even married them, a fact that made my cousin clench his fists. In the city, integration required money.

Aware of this, I husbanded that which was still mine. Without telling my cousin, I held back the remnants of my handsome send-off, using it to purchase a savings certificate. But nothing would restore me to the privilege I had enjoyed, failing to realize how extraordinary it was, when I sat in a dormitory room in Thunder Bay and stared across flickering candles into the eyes of Shelley or Melissa. If I had followed that path, if I had *struggled* to complete my B.A., though the thought of such exertions appalled me, I might have become Canadian. Vowing not to succumb to nostalgia, I muffled my memories. I muffled everything and became no one.

FIVE
desperate remedies

As celibate as the Mahatma, I found that celibacy
deepened my indolence. Eight years passed. The
1970s, the decade of my youth, yielded to the
1980s. My revered England, like tortured India,
fell under the rule of a woman of iron. America
was led by an actor; in Canada, the prime minister who had said that the state had no place in the
bedrooms of the nation lost power briefly, then
returned, strengthening the newspapers' conviction that Canada was exempt from the torments
that rocked the world.

I might never have rediscovered myself had
it not been for my eldest brother. One day the
phone rang and I heard the voice of the left-armed
fast bowler, who now knocked over wickets

on the Bombay stock exchange. "Our father is not getting younger," he said. "You would know that if you had returned in February with the rest of the rabble ... He wants to see you settled. Do you need capital to invest in a business? Why are you not married? You're not a poofter, are you?"

"I ..."

"What is it you want, R. U.?"

I held my breath. My dormant instinct for opportunity, muted by eight years of grovelling for jobs, warned me this might be my last chance. A fifth son must bow to an eldest son. Any reader of Victorian novels knows that.

"We need to make a respectable man of you. You know what they say here, don't you? They say that girlie magazine they caught you with was a ruse and you went away because you have tendencies. Remember when you were a child and played dress-up like a girl? They're saying that was evidence—"

"I certainly do have tendencies—"

"I knew it! I'm not going to support that. You don't belong in our family. You debase us, R. U. You can just fuck off—"

I allowed him to work himself into a fury, then I let him have it between the eyes. "I have

tendencies towards the seduction of white wom-
en. It's a weakness I can't satisfy in India. It drives
me mad."

"I'll wager they don't let you near them." For
the first time, his voice betrayed hesitation.

"On the contrary—" I detailed my Thunder
Bay conquests by name, by blonde or brunette,
by clear skin or freckles, by leg and breast; I gave
him to understand that I continued to pursue
such lasciviousness.

When one is poor, one is never alone: my
cousin and his flatmates were watching a film that
starred the Bollywood actress Helen, their ideal
of pure Indian beauty. They muted the film to
eavesdrop on my salaciousness with expressions
of satisfied disgust. I had never been so foolish
as to share my triumphs with them. Now I was
on the razor's edge. After hearing this, my cousin
would eject me from the apartment and his community. Unless I extracted a pay-off from my
brother, I would be out on the street.

"You're a pervert!" My brother's affection was
unmistakable. The left-armed fast bowler was a
champion of patriarchy and heteronormativity.
"You do it with white women? How could you?
I say, brother, I've always thought you were a

tremendous fellow. Now tell me. What is it you want in life? What line of work do you want to go into?"

I thought so hard that I began to sweat. I knew that if I tried to run a business, I would run it into the ground. If I applied myself, I could complete a degree in literature. But to find a job, I would have to speak of literature as Canadian professors did, and on one point I was certain: no group's thinking was more muddled than that of Canadian professors. I thought: *a squire*, and heard the half rhyme with *lawyer*. A lawyer in rural Canada … I envisaged an idyllic hamlet where I would be unique and picturesque rather than common and ghettoized.

"How much does law school cost in Canada?" my brother asked.

His question initiated a period of negotiation, punctuated by phone calls and letters and application forms. I became aloof from my cousin and his flatmates. To them, I had become immoral. I did not respect my community; I was a bad influence on young people. Fortunately, the cost of law school in Canada remained reasonable.

In September I left Toronto.

I cashed in my savings certificate to buy a Lada

that had been slewing over Canada's snowy roads since before my arrival in Thunder Bay. The day I stowed my clothes in the back seat and my books in the boot, and bid farewell to my cousin and his roommates, who clamoured that I was unclean and they would slam the door in my face when I came crawling back to them, I knew my tribulations were over. I could consign those years to memory as a blur of ordeals endured. Just as stout Englishmen had returned from the North-West Frontier or the source of the Nile to the comforts of London clubs, so I was returning to the society that soothed me.

As I drove west, past turnoffs to towns with names from English history, I realized I was going to London, as I had dreamed of doing. Like me, this London had shed any pretensions to the authenticity of the original. Rather than fog, I was bathed in sunshine. The city looked like a suburb, the grim little downtown emptied at 5 p.m., but the university campus, with its grandiose sandstone gates and nineteenth-century tower, filled me with confidence that here were people like myself: people of no particular distinction who were in the process of acquiring distinction— or a convincing veneer of it, which was what mattered. Though many of my classmates came from wealthy families, the pitch of my accent and my capacity for literary allusions made them treat me with circumspection. These budding lawyers from families that had money and yearned for culture knew they were in the presence of an erudite fellow. Had they glimpsed me unloading a truck at a big box store, they would have written me off as a Paki; here they deferred to me. I let my beard grow. The day I arrived and moved into my rented room, I took my turban downstairs to the laundry room and washed it and my turban cap. Later, I practised folding them again, letting the little tail dangle down the back of my neck. I wrapped the cloth around my head, then wrapped it again. My conscious mind had forgotten this sequence of gestures, but my hands remembered. When I looked in the mirror, a handsome fellow in a bright blue turban, perfectly tucked, stared back at me. His beard was still scraggly, but time would take care of that.

In conversations at pubs after class (I ordered wine, my classmates preferred Guinness) I explained that Sikh men took the name Singh in rejection of distinctions of caste and class. The crown of my turban lent my declarations a princely authority, enhanced now by a body that was fuller than it had been in my Lakehead days. My disquisitions gained me a progressive following in a conservative university. More than that: they earned me a girlfriend. Intimidated by my need to struggle—an indignity, I now grasped, that would open the door to a dignified life—I had not sought a girlfriend. I had promised myself, and more importantly, had promised the left-armed fast bowler, that I would work to justify my family's confidence in me. A third degree to which "(failed)" was appended would condemn me to life imprisonment in the towers beyond the end of the subway line.

I had hoped for other Shelleys or Melissas. As I allowed myself a little cautious activism, sufficient to establish myself as an open-minded fellow, without distracting myself from exams or being labelled as a hothead, I rubbed shoulders with women of passion and commitment. Before long, I was an object of passion, a partner in commitment. The apparatus of seduction—wine, candles—was hers, not mine. The left-armed fast bowler would have said that by allowing a woman to take such initiative I was not behaving like a man, yet how he would have envied the manly outcome of my unmanliness! By relinquishing patriarchy, I quaffed from the chalice of hetero-normativity.

I was nervous on my first night with Esther. (Yes, my beloved was Jewish. Her grandparents had fled Czarist Russia as communists. I was impressed. At two generations' remove, communism is a form of aristocracy.) I knew I must conceal how many years had passed since my last intimate experience with a woman: she could regard my long celibacy only as evidence of failure. Once you begin to mingle with future lawyers, you cannot allow even your beloved to suspect that you have ever failed at anything. The ethos of my new community would oblige Esther to spurn me if I revealed myself as less than a practised, ha-bitual lover. I was surprised to discover that this troubled me: hadn't I been seeking a tryst? Yet in the shadow of the tower that dominated the campus of this London of the provinces, sliding in and out of women's bodies was no longer suf-ficient: to secure my position, I must anchor my-self in an enduring connection.

The extent of my anxiety took me by surprise. It drove my perceptions inward, honing my con-sciousness of my body as our clothes dropped to the floor in a dishevelled embrace. I reminded myself that the act in which I was about to engage was a series of gestures. Like culture, love was the product of deft movements. When our lovemaking began in earnest, I realized that now I was over thirty, the vein-searing climaxes of my early youth had cooled. My body expanded to fill the room; hers became invisible. I longed for the easy pleasure I had taken in Thunder Bay, my wide-eyed tourism of white female flesh. Morose in the aftermath of passion as I lamented the waning responsiveness of my nerve-ends—a waning, I was certain, I scarcely would have noticed on a day-by-day basis, but which an eight-year hiatus had thrown into jagged relief—I confronted with painful clarity the years of pleasure that had been quashed by my cousin's community.

Having returned to my body, I lavished attention on Esther. Even as I did so, my attention felt as trumped-up as a politician's palaver. Yet she seemed charmed; perhaps verbosity was what she expected from her cultured Indian? She asked me how she differed in bed from Indian girls. It was clear that by "differed from" she meant "was better than." I flattered her, concealing that I had no experience of Indian girls, that such experience

43

was not normally available to an unmarried Indian man. I told her that with her hooded eyelids, dark hair, and slightly olive skin, she could pass for a Kashmiri girl. She told me that my beard scratched and aroused her as though she were making love with a Talmudic prophet. Like my cousin, Esther asserted her membership in a community.

My classmates did not grasp the predicament of being a fifth son in a country where rules cannot be breached, of lifting the phone late at night and hearing the left-armed fast bowler demanding a full accounting of my grades. "You are studying as your father's son! You must honour our family!"

Esther laughed when I told her of these calls. "Your brother," she said, "sounds like my father."

She invited me to meet her parents.

44

the hamlet

Esther and I became one of the law school's recognized couples. The fact of our being together,
though I myself had not thought of it in this way,
was seen as a political statement: an emblem of
multiculturalism and Canadian tolerance, a challenge to the bland, white assumptions of London,
Ontario. I was noticed, I was respected. Realizing
that any word I uttered would only blemish my
status, I avoided risky declarations. Preferring the
security of silence, I cultivated the mien of the inscrutable Oriental. I adopted this pose even with
Esther's parents. When we went to dinner at their
house, in one of the Toronto neighbourhoods
where rich Indians fraternized with whites, my
return to the city unnerved me, as though I were

revisiting the scene of a trauma. I boxed up my agitation in long, thoughtful silences. At the end of the evening, Esther told me that I had made a good impression. As we drove back to London, with the lorries swooping past us in the darkness, I said: "They didn't seem worried that you might have Indian children."

"They know," Esther said, "that any children I have will be Jewish."

"Because Jewishness passes through the mother?"

"Because I wouldn't let them not be Jewish, silly!"

I stared ahead over the steering wheel as a lorry shot past in the outer lane and vanished into the darkness. "How foolish of me not to think of that," I murmured.

This conversation sowed the seeds of a disquiet whose slow germination over the next three years condemned us not to marry. Not that I feared Jewish children: I would have welcomed them. My fear was that, like most Canadians, Esther underestimated unassimilated cultures. Any children I had would be Indian sons. I would beget repetitions of my brothers. For all its Jewish tenacity, Esther's third-generation Canadian tolerance wouldn't stand a chance against the ancient intransigence I would transmit to our offspring. My children would resemble the left-armed fast bowler.

I never wished to encounter such beings.

Nor did I wish to return to Toronto. My provincial ideal was within reach. Once I was a lawyer, I would be able to settle in a village and hang out my sign. I could earn a living on the side while devoting myself to cultured pursuits. I could take walks along the river and through the park, and be recognized by my fellow village professionals as a gentleman of property and culture. Esther, though, was committed to alleviating the plight of immigrants: this was integral to her commitment to me (it was unclear which was cause and which effect), her commitment to her society, and her reverence for her refugee grandparents. To sacrifice her earning potential on the altar of immigration law, she would have to go work in Toronto; I refused to return there. Our classmates, who exulted as they lined up articling jobs with Bay Street law firms, thought we had both lost our minds.

We no longer wanted the same things.

I graduated from law school and did my

articling with a small firm in London. Having suppressed my past failures, I was now *B.A. Bombay, LL.B. Western*. I no longer had a girlfriend.

My articling passed in a flurry of long nights that wore me out. By the time I passed the bar exam, I was ready to repair to the countryside. For a week, I drove around southern Ontario in my dilapidated Lada in search of a likely village. That was how I met the woman who would make and break my fugitive's life. A woman whom I took to be the core of Canadianness, yet who turned out to be an immigrant more desperate for acceptance than I was. A woman who was not a lover, but something even more alluring: a transfixing mentor.

I stopped in an old Scottish mill town. Nineteenth-century chipped limestone walls dived straight into a ravine where water swirled after plunging over rapids, then ran deep and black towards the weir that sucked it downstream. I sauntered uphill. The main street had cafés and shops that sold souvenirs and local baking, a post office, a quaint old city hall, and a grocery. Branching out on either side were leisurely quarters where houses, some of them built of red brick and others of the pale local limestone, sat on broad, sloping lawns. Maple trees reached to the sky. This was the home I had imagined. It was an English village built by Scots in Canada. The layered residue of a British colonial history that I shared renewed my spirits, assuring me that here, in contrast to my cousin's tower—in contrast, even, to an authentic village in England's Home Counties—I would find a congenial home. I walked around every block of the residential area, then returned to a corner where a high hedge screened a bevy of conversation. I heard the splattering of a fountain and the rise and fall of voices.

I stepped through a gap in the hedge and entered a garden party. I glimpsed the labels on the wine bottles that stood, more empty than full, on a long wooden table fit for a medieval feast. The word *Château* abounded. Very fine taste was evident here. The people were older than me, in bohemian middle age. The women wore their grey hair loose. Their earrings were oversized and struck from dull gold. One man had mutton-chop sideburns; another, who spoke with the accent of an overseas English colonialist, wore the uneven beard of a sensitive swashbuckler. Their clothes were of nonchalant elegance: loose-fitting silk dresses, bright dress shirts. Mine, fortunately, were formal: taken by the notion that I might apply for a lease, I had put on a grey suit and a pale turban.

The people who sat along the table looked uncomfortable at my entrance, not because I was Indian, but simply because they seemed accustomed to living in clusters where they never met anyone whom they did not know already. The woman at the head of the table was different. Her eyes were hard with the insights of a survivor. Her swoop of blond hair was unmarred; unlike the others, she had not allowed herself to go grey. I saw that she was the hostess and that the tall, shambling man with the ragged white mane who roamed the yard with an oversized wine glass in his hand was her husband. I perceived in that moment that the bond between husband and wife was elastic, allowing ample space for others in their lives. All of this was clear to me at a glance, with a prescience that reinforced my conviction that I had come home. Though these people exuded wealth and sophistication, the hostess frightened me. I knew in a second that she was my challenge and the pivot of my acceptance: if I could win her over, I would belong to this group.

I stepped towards her.

"Well, how do you do?" she said. "I didn't know there was anyone like you in this town."

"Milly," a frizzy-haired woman said in a gravel voice. "Mind your p's and q's."

"I live here. I know the locals. Are you from Toronto?"

"From London," I said.

"London, England, I assume." The swashbuckler's droll Englishness made it unclear whether he was speaking in jest.

"I'm moving here." I opted for ambiguity. "I act for, talk for, live for this world now."

"Robert Browning!" the bearded man said. "Don't tell me you're a writer?"

"I'm a lawyer," I said. "A lawyer with a B.A. and M.A. in English literature from Bombay."

"And you're moving here?" the hostess said. "You and I must get to know each other."

She made room for me next to her at the head of the long table. I sat down, conscious that these were the sort of people who would prize my picturesqueness as evidence of what Canadians referred to as their tolerance. They greeted me with uncertain smiles, undermined by a half-fearful condescension. The hostess, who introduced herself as Millicent Crowe, poured me a glass of one of the finer Châteaux.

We clinked glasses. Our bond was sealed.

We talked until the others had left for Toronto in their Mercedes and BMWs. They lavished Milly with hugs and kisses, and proffered me handshakes. Milly's husband slid back the French door and disappeared into the house. "He writes best after a couple of drinks," she murmured. The fountain splashed behind us. "I hope you appreciate that you've been in the company of some of Canada's finest writers." As she spoke the words, going on to retail the names of each of her guests, her voice made clear that she was offering me a gift and it was incumbent on me to feel gratitude for her bounty.

"I'm grateful," I hastened to say. "I must confess that I'm more acquainted with Dickens or Trollope …"

"I'll write down their names. You will need to inform yourself if you're to join us. Don't stop reading Victorian literature, though. Your ability to quote Browning is charming."

Milly and I spoke until evening crept in, and her husband returned to the yard with a distracted air to turn off the fountain. Milly, I learned, was an immigrant, too, albeit of a more subtle shade than I: she was a professor from the southern United States who had come north with her husband fifteen years earlier out of opposition to the Vietnam War. She told me she was related to the family of John Crowe Ransom.

I drove back to London in the dark. The next day I went to the public library, looked up John Crowe Ransom, and learned that he was a literary critic who had belonged to a group called the Fugitives. They had styled themselves agrarian aristocrats. As I read these words, my breast filled with warmth. I had found my home, my community, as my cousin would have said. The communities that mattered, I thought, imagining myself at long last winning an argument with him, were those you chose rather than those that were mandated by a language, a religion, or a shade of skin. I visited a bookstore and bought novels by two of the writers I had met in Milly's garden. I was mildly disappointed to learn that they were not agrarian aristocrats. They wrote books set in cities or in far-away countries, such as mine. The paperback editions of their novels attested to their fame. A tremor strummed my chest. Never before—not even with Esther's parents, and certainly not with my Lakehead paramours had I felt closer to my new country's core. As I prepared to return to the village that held my future, a hovering heat unsettled me, like the crowding sensation I had felt when I first desired Esther. As I thought about Milly, a pool of desire, promising fulfillment, spread before me. As nervous as an adolescent, I lifted the receiver of my phone and rang her number. Her husband answered like a gruff parent. I asked for his wife.

"Who the hell are you?" the husband asked.

"This is R. U. Singh, attorney at law."

Milly took the phone. We arranged to meet for coffee late in the afternoon. Milly was a vice-president at a university in a small city half an hour away. She would return to the village only at three-thirty.

I drove up in the morning. By noon I had rented a spacious flat that overlooked the river. It was on the second floor of a bakery that also contained the village's most popular riverside café. The warm sweet-bread smell from below softened the susurration of the rapids. The mid-morning light spun into the living room in swirls that reflected the gyrations of black water as it was expelled from the rapids and sloughed towards the weir. I was a lawyer now, and, almost its half rhyme, a squire, possessed of a dwelling of rural splendour, if not of land. My flat had a private entrance by way of an outdoor staircase.

Wandering the streets, I found a hardware store that made signs. I ordered a sign that would read: R. U. *Singh, Attorney at Law. B.A., M.A., LL.B., Q.C.* My success at law school and on the bar exam having redeemed me, a point even the left-armed fast bowler conceded, I saw no reason to suppress my maligned M.A. It was in an M.A. seminar, for which I had neglected to hand in the essay, that I had memorized a few lines of Browning's "Bishop Blougram's Apology." In the most direct way, my M.A., failed or not, had transported me to this place that would complete my destiny. Failures, too, can become successes: the successful man may claim them, in their inverse identity, as the foundations of his education.

Milly and I met in the bakery café by the river; the other customers were visitors from Toronto who had driven out for the day to savour colonial Ontario. Without having spent my first night in the village, I was already able to distinguish tourists from locals. The tourists looked around with curiosity at the limestone walls and the woven wall hangings; the locals read the copies of the

Toronto Star and *Globe and Mail* that the owners scattered over the tables. I counted myself among the rustics as I sat in a corner where the wainscotting had been stripped away to expose pitted limestone.

The blue-jeaned waitress brushed past a batik-patterned rectangle of fabric to emerge from the kitchen. I was contemplating this scrap of Indian culture adopted by the West, seeing in it a banner that announced my own good fortune, when Milly came in the door. Her thick hair billowed on her shoulders like that of a younger woman, conveying vigour and conviction. Having arrived straight from the university, she was dressed like a vice-president: a navy blue skirt and matching blazer over a white blouse, low-heeled black pumps, a discreet gold necklace. The owner, who looked like the waitress's father, greeted her with subdued respect. We ordered green tea and what, in childhood, I had learned to call a sticky bun. When I told Milly that I had begun to read her friends' work, her eyes concentrated on me in a way that made them look smaller.

"You can be of value to those people, R. U. It would be in my interest and very much in yours." Her smile belonged to a goddess who requires no

sustenance from humans. "You have to understand, they're Canadian—"

"I have been trying to decipher the riddle of
Canadianness for many years," I said, with a smile
that I hoped was serene.

"Well, I've solved it, and you're part of the
solution." As she spoke of her dismay that those
qualities the United States had ranked as her
best—drive, ambition, outspokenness—were
seen in Canada as social gaffes, I perceived all that
Milly and I had in common. Her allusions to the
Deep South, which stirred memories of my assiduous reading of William Faulkner, made clear
that in that society of encrusted social distinctions she had inhabited an echelon near the top.
I spoke of the Academy and of my father, giving
her to understand that I, too, came from the pinnacle of a caste society. Like her, I was an immigrant who knew himself to be socially superior to
the people whose favours he must earn.

"Isn't it rich that *they* decide *our* fates?" she said.
"In Canada, R. U., you must always be cautious.
The United States and India are big enough for
people to disappear into other lives. In Canada anyone you deal with will cross your path again, so be
careful how you treat them. And they are *all* needy.

They need to be seen as open, liberal, and worldly, yet they're terrified of leaving their little cages. If you drag them out into the open, they will finish you off." I realized that she was speaking of her friends. "Canada has shifted beneath their feet. They need multicultural friends but don't know where to find them. Without them, they'll look out of touch—"

"You have taken it upon yourself to save them," I said, eager to confirm that I was a fellow who was not slow on the uptake. I laid my hands on the oak tabletop, where, next to Milly's bony, manicured pallor, they looked not only dark, but of a meaty thickness.

"As I told you," she said, with a briskness that betrayed impatience, "it will benefit you and it will benefit me."

"It will benefit you by consolidating your friendship with famous writers?"

"I like to have literary friends …"

Surprised by her uncharacteristic hesitation, I asked her: "You're a writer?"

A long pause. She pursed her mouth, throwing into relief half-submerged wrinkles. "When I was young, I thought I would be a writer. Growing up in that atmosphere: John Crowe Ransom, the Fugitives ... I married a writer. But my own writing, well. Then I thought I would write literary criticism like my illustrious relative. I got a Ph.D., but I never published as much as I should have. It turns out that what I'm good at is organizing programs, getting people to do what I want by giving them what they think they want, being a dean and a vice-president. But I can't face being just that. I need to be in the thick of literary life. That's how I was reared."

Her head peered into her earthenware coffee mug. "I have similar feelings," I said, hoping to soften this moment of discomfort.

"You know you're special, R. U.? I don't tell everyone these things."

Her wide mouth appealed for allegiance. Her eyes measured my reaction, assessing whether she was gaining full benefit from her confession. Milly was truly an expert in inducing people to feel what she needed them to feel. I sensed her calculation, even as the obligation to cherish her moment of weakness as evidence of our intimacy, and to be loyal to her, enlisted me as her follower.

I admired her ability to make me feel what she wanted me to feel. There was undeniable art in it.

"My husband and I are accustomed to a certain

style in our life," she murmured. "Yet I'm the sole breadwinner. Without style, you don't attract eminent people. I need that fountain in my yard!"

"Your husband is not employed?"

"He writes and he drinks. His books earn very little. He's too American for Canada, and he's been away from the South for too long for folks down home to remember him. He makes a little money by travelling around and giving readings and picking up his reading fees." She put down her mug. "I just wish his fees were all he picked up!"

Sensing another difficult moment, I remained silent. The maw of that terrifying beast, the long-term Western marriage, gaped before my eyes. Esther had recounted the rise and fall and rise again of her parents' union. She remembered their playfulness when she was a child, the tension and distance (and, she suspected, affairs) of her teenage years, the reconciliation, and then a kind of leathery endurance that was a fossilized skeleton of love, ingrained with the harsh knowledge, droll understanding, and pragmatic financial partnership of incipient old age. She had held up this portrait to me as though it were a yardstick against which to measure our future.

No matter how Canadian I might become, I would never understand this sort of marriage. I knew I did not want the other sort of marriage, which my cousin and roommates in the towers had sought in their quest for devout virgins who, with a discreet hand from ultrasound machines and willing doctors, would give birth to male offspring only. More Indian sons! The thought chilled me.

Esther, with her frankness, had made me more worldly. Yet there are conversations in which a man born in Bombay does not participate. Discussing the extramarital affairs of a woman's husband with the lady herself is one of them.

"I don't want you to think," Milly said, as my silence grew uncomfortable, "that I let him get away with it. Sometimes when he comes home from one of his gigs and what happened is written all over his face, that hangdog face of his gets one hell of a slap!"

I winced, as though I were the recipient of her blow. "Does that cure him?"

"When it doesn't," she whispered, "I go to bed with another man!"

This was a marriage? I felt relieved that my

romance with Esther had not led to matrimony. Yet I could see that Milly and her husband were inseparable. Inscrutable Occidentals! Who can fathom their opaque depths?

Milly's smile tightened. "Do you have affairs, R. U.?"

In what I hoped was a composed tone, I said: "I have had a number of affairs. At law school, I had a Canadian girlfriend whom I nearly married."

"I'll keep you in mind the next time I need to get my revenge." She smiled to signal that this was a joke: a smile whose predatory mirth showed, at the same time, that it was not a joke. I was anxious to hold complications at bay. "What I seek from you is a different form of solace."

She leaned back in her chair. I glimpsed a shadow of hatred in her resignation. Millicent Crowe did not accept rejection. Even if she did not wish to go to bed with me, she required me to hunger to go to bed with her. In every relationship, it must be she who held the upper hand: every relationship except, perhaps, her incessant struggle with her husband. Yet I did not wish to be an exotic conquest, swiftly discarded. I refused to be relegated like a faltering football team demoted to the fourth division. I wanted my presence in her life, my availability to receive her social favours, to be eternal. Our relationship must remain unresolved: it must be a flirtation that always promised but never delivered, a climax that was forever coming but never came. I must never allow the tension between us to dissipate.

In a throaty voice, Milly asked: "What kind of solace are you looking for, R. U.?"

"In reality I place no limits on it. Only on the temporal boundaries in which it may occur."

She gave me a long, cruel, appreciative look. "Maybe it's better if I don't have an affair with you. You'd be more unbearable than my husband."

She gave my hand a long caress, as though to show that she could. I felt like her mascot, her son, her adolescent boyfriend.

Whenever she chatted with me on the phone, I knew that her high-spirited garrulousness was for the benefit of the brooding husband who listened in the next room. While I prolonged the tenure of my inclusion in her social circle, she teased her husband with my interest in her, and hers in me. I kept talking, confident that in its tensed equilibrium, this conversation would nourish me for years.

SEVEN
the way we live now

Once my sign had arrived, and I had hung it at
the bottom of the staircase, my life paused. No
clients appeared; no income entered my chequing
account. My historic mill town already had lawyers: a crusty old gentleman who had completed
every local property transfer in the last thirty
years, and a drunken middle-aged wretch who did
divorces and threats of lawsuits between sparring
neighbours (rumour claimed that he preferred to
represent both parties). Between them, these two
colleagues absorbed the bulk of the village's legal
traffic. For all the beauty of its colonial architecture, my new home was not large enough to support what my law-school classmates referred to
as a boutique firm. My days were spent reading

the books of my new literary acquaintances; the nights were harder. I asked myself how I would pay the rent in three months' time.

I wondered whether not marrying Esther had been a mistake. I longed for company such as I had enjoyed in my capsule-like dormitory room. I wondered whether Seema had married. My loneliness instilled lethargy, sapping me of the energy that might have allowed me to go out and drum up business, had I been so inclined. To tell the truth, I was not much inclined. Drumming up business sounded like a struggle. Having successfully completed law school, I'd had my fill of struggle.

Milly saved me. She delighted in aiding cases like mine, those of cultured layabouts, particularly those who promised to enrich her friends' multicultural credentials. I had begun to understand that in Canada, as I supposed the left-armed fast bowler would tell me was also the case in Bombay, knowing the right people brought money within reach. Milly asked me if I would be willing to serve as the trustee for donations to a literary prize that her friends were organizing in Toronto. My work would be pro bono, but my photograph would appear in the newspaper.

Cheques arrived in the mail. I held them in escrow, then drove to Toronto, my Lada barely able to complete the journey. At a meal with dinner jackets and flashing cameras, I announced the total that had been donated, and handed a cheque to one of Milly's smiling writer friends. The evening's program announced that the prize money was held by "R. U. Singh, Q.C., a southwestern Ontario lawyer." The swashbuckler and the woman with the gravel voice smiled with satisfaction as certain well-dressed white people stopped short at the sight of the southwestern Ontario lawyer. They revelled in their superior knowledge that a person described in this way might be a brown man in a turban, whose black beard contained flickers of grey resembling fire tamped down into ash. With proprietary nods the writers assumed the new sheen I had brought to their reputations. Their admirers beat a path towards me. Among them were various journalists.

Following the practice I had adopted in law school—now my Canadian education came to my aid—I avoided risky declarations, turning questions back on the questioner with avuncular irony. I threaded my declarations with references to my reading. I told one journalist that I felt like one of the outsiders who flock to the heart of Victorian society in late Trollope novels, such as *The Way We Live Now*. The interviews were my contribution to literature. The next week, Milly brought me clippings from newspapers and magazines in which my photograph appeared and my words were cited. "You were magnificent," she said, gasping from climbing my stairs.

"I am always pleased when a breathless woman pays me that compliment."

I was learning how to entertain her. We sat down to have a drink; I, too, had begun to keep a stock of expensive wine. She told me the score from her husband's reading tour of the Maritimes.

"Two undergraduates and one conference organizer," she said with drawling precision. "That's what he's confessed to, anyway."

Having learned to avoid blunt statements, I was now a better listener. My career, though recognized now, was not yet generating income. I drew up wills for two village residents; this paid only another month's rent. Despondency set in. The summer ended and with the first cold nights, a mist of Holmesian density, yet twice as chilly as any in Sherlock's London, lofted up off the river below my apartment. Milly was busy at the university. Esther got in touch to let me know that she was marrying and—far more hurtful—that she had given up immigration law and the men it had brought her way. Her fiancé, who had proposed to her on a beach in Israel, was the son of friends of her parents. She was working at a corporate law firm called Davies, which, because of the exorbitant hours it demanded of its employees, was known in the profession as Slaveys. As Esther worked late at a tower on Bay Street, I sat reading in the silence of my apartment. My Lada coughed its last burst of exhaust. Having paid to have it towed away, I was both impoverished and trapped. No longer a squire, I was a pedestrian peasant.

At the point where my despair had dipped down deeper than the bottom of the river, my telephone rang. A pale, stifled Toronto voice invited me to join the board of a charitable organization. Board members had been present, I was told, on the night of the southwestern Ontario lawyer's appearance in Toronto; they had been impressed by my *suavity*—this was the word he used—and, to be frank, he said, their board was in need of *diversity*. I accepted before I could wonder how I would get to Toronto for the board's four annual meetings, and also before I realized that such posts came with what were known as retainers. In return for reading files and being ready to discuss them, I would receive ten thousand dollars a year.

From this point, though money arrived by fits and starts separated by hiatuses that were long enough to make me fret, I knew I would not starve. I went into debt to buy a reliable second-hand car; I spent certain nights in Toronto, where I had met Chyou, a slender widow from Shanghai who owned two manicure and pedicure shops. Urgency drifted out of my life, as did the hope of conspicuous success. When the left-armed fast bowler phoned to boast of his latest corporate merger, I found myself on the defensive. He didn't care that I knew everyone who mattered in the literary world of puny Toronto. Yet I cared. Never had I loitered so magnificently in the garden of loiterature. Millicent Crowe's fountain splattered all summer, in a dulled, syncopated echo of the sloshing of the rapids outside my window. That summer I was reading Marcel Proust. Milly became my Duchess of Guermantes: the dazzling hostess who bestowed an illustrious shimmer on society, purging experience of drab dailyness. Milly's literary friends arrived, with their casual yet shimmering clothes, accompanied by famous writers from New York or London or Paris or Buenos Aires who were eager to cast an eye on Canadian rusticity—the rusticity of a beautiful, enclosed garden behind a renovated nineteenth-century house, where Toronto's illuminati and France's finest vintages were married for their delectation. The local colour—in more senses than they had perhaps anticipated—was provided by R. U. Singh, the southwestern Ontario lawyer. A lawyer, it must be said, whose client portfolio remained meagre; but who had acquired three charitable directorships, each of which provided an annual retainer.

My means were modest. When I took my widow out on the town, I squandered money I should have been saving. I brought Chyou to the village only once, on a day when Milly was at the university. I intimated to Milly that I had a lover in Toronto, yet did not go into details. It was a fine balance. I feared Milly's defection if I made her the confidante for my delights and doubts. If I angered her, I would never again step inside the garden. My rural financial viability, and the squire's existence it brought me, would trickle away, obliging me to move and become

simply one more Toronto lawyer. Had I hidden
my lover from Milly, she would have found me
out: she knew everyone's secrets. Even if she had
not discovered me, to appear sexless would have
diminished my allure. For our bantering to continue yielding fruit, I had to appear desirable: not
a cipher, but a man of the world who had women
in his bed. As in every aspect of this anti-marriage
between two high-caste refugees, I must keep the
sheen of my desirability well buffed. Actual sex
with Milly would bring my village life to an abrupt
end; banishing all intimations of sex would have
the same result. It was in an intermediate zone of
endless enticement and eternally open erotic conversation that Milly and I tantalized each other.

I sat beside her at the head of the table as the
writers vented their anger at all that offended
them in the literary world, and in the nation.
Milly helped them devise campaigns against de-
structive policies. In law school, where I had
learned so much more than the law, I had become
accustomed to the idea that in Canada the pursuit
of a cultured life went hand-in-hand not with the
conservative politics of an aristocrat, as I had believed in my youth, but with those of nationalism
and social democracy. When, during one of our

early conversations, I had expressed my passion for Rudyard Kipling, Milly had hushed me. As a visible minority, she said, I could never divulge such sympathies.

I grasped that Milly had gone through a process that I must emulate, exchanging her aristocratic elitism for a more liberal variety to secure her Canadian friendships. As time went on, the vestiges of my aristocratic impulses withered away: the longer I lived in the village, the clearer it was where my interests lay. I resolved to say little, to absorb in silence the assumptions that were expressed around me.

One afternoon, I listened with care as Milly offered the writers counsel on how they should refute a notorious literary troublemaker who had attacked their friends. The key, she said, was to outflank him. By the end of the afternoon it had been decided that they would enlist a young woman writer from Nova Scotia's Annapolis Valley to refute this thug. In this way, the riposte would not appear as a wounded howl from the privileged heart of Toronto, but as a balanced argument made by a popular young woman in a national context. The young woman, it was decided, would be rewarded by being named a finalist for a national literary award. As always, Milly's strategy worked. The thug was discredited; his publishing opportunities dried up and he was not heard from again. The young woman became quite famous.

Politicians, by contrast, were more difficult to vanquish. Though I did not say so—not saying what one thought was essential to developing a Canadian personality—I considered it a sign of poor taste for artists to meddle in political debate. Yet Milly's friends regarded art as inseparable from national identity. I was familiar with this tendency from India; there I had opposed it. Politics had no place in the life of a literary squire. Milly was better than I at responding to these activist enthusiasms. She brought her administrative acumen to the writers' campaigns. I—and I alone, I suspected—discerned the downward thrust of the bunched wrinkles in the corner of her mouth. In her life as an administrative infighter, she had confided to me over coffee, it fell to her to do many distasteful things. She was prepared to use the same ruthlessness to make herself indispensable to her friends.

I did not reflect then on the implications of this statement.

EIGHT
the prime minister

The fountain doused the stones in happy cacophony in the late summer afternoon. The swashbuckler recounted tales of the Orient, observing me with an eye at once complicit and wary. My senses enlarged, yet their sharpness diminished, by Pinot Grigio (Niagara Peninsula variety), I played along with his fabrications in a way that may have been forced. He changed the subject to Canadian politics. Milly's husband, who had returned from Winnipeg the night before, remained quiet. After decades in Canada, he had as little understanding of the country's politics as my cousin.

The writers were deploring the prime minister. Unable to push a tax on books, among other items, through a Senate that remained top-heavy with politicians who belonged to the party of Her Majesty's Loyal Opposition, the prime minister had announced a unilateral enlargement of the Senate. He was adding new senators from his own party to create a majority that would make books cost more.

"He always was an utter prick," the swashbuckler said, impatient to return to his monologue.

"This is different than being a prick," the woman with the gravel voice replied. "This is weakening culture."

"It wouldn't stand up to a legal challenge," the man with the sideburns of a Kiplingesque colonel said.

"A legal challenge!" The idea made Milly shine. She drew herself upright at the head of the long oak table.

"It couldn't come from us," the gravel-voiced woman said. "You know what the papers would say——"

"Exactly. We need that girl from Nova Scotia again. The challenge must come from a source who is indisputably autonomous—from the new Canada, not the old!"

Had I drunk less, I would have been wary.

Or eager. My bleary perceptions made it difficult to discern whether I was on the brink of triumph or disaster. They were all looking at me. I glanced at Milly. For her, for the love of loiterature, I would consider taking on this knight errant's errand, this fool's commission. Feeling like a young woman scrutinizing her suitor, I wondered whether I could trust her. "If I do it," I said, "if it goes wrong, will you come to my aid?"

"We're not in India, you know," the swashbuckler said.

"There is always danger in attacking a sitting government. A prime minister who is willing to break the law to change the Senate can easily destroy a defenceless immigrant."

"You're not defenceless, R. U.," Milly said. "We're behind you."

I looked down the table. In their blank-faced expressions, I saw not a promise but a threat: the fugitive must pay the price of his asylum. As I observed this group of Canadians, for whom directness was a way of never saying what they thought—because to do so was in poor taste, because it might be held against them if the mood changed—I realized how precarious was my squire's life. These people did not possess the authority to banish me to my cousin's tower, and yet, I felt, they did. Without their advocacy, I would not be drawing my retainers on charitable boards. Was I being paranoid, as Milly said of her enemies at the university? The terror that crawled up my spine came from not being certain, from not possessing an intuitive understanding, as I might have had in my own country—yes, in that dangerous moment I felt that India, not Canada, was my country—of how people could be expected to act.

"Aren't you a Canadian citizen?" a lanky, patrician man, who attended Milly's garden gatherings when he was not in Africa or Asia, dining with dictators or roaming the bush with guerrillas, said. "All citizens are equal. No one can touch you."

The others smiled in self-satisfaction. I glimpsed their certainty that all was right in Canada, that their country was an exception to humanity's corruptions, was unique in its tolerance, and, above all, was demonstrably superior in every respect to the putrefying United States of America. I glanced in the direction of Milly, my fellow outsider. Her face rebuffed my claim to intimacy. She was in disguise as a Canadian, repudiating the experience that she and I shared. Behind her back, her husband prowled the yard, unable

to feign interest in the incident that was unfold-
ing at the table. His incomprehension made me
realize how much I understood. I did not want a
tax on books, either. I acted for, talked for, lived
for this world now. My anger merging with that
of my friends, I murmured: "I want to stop this.
The freedom to read is sacred."

"Do it for your country!" Milly said, pounc-
ing on my uncomfortable silence.

I hated her with the hatred one feels for a lover
who has committed a betrayal. In that instant,
we were a couple. Startled by the force of feeling
that cuffed me across the shoulders like a brusque
schoolmaster, I got to my feet. Chyou, my seduc-
tress of the manicures and pedicures, had never
aroused me as Milly did in that second. Realizing that I was on the verge of being repelled, and
that I must reclaim her, I stood up. "I'll do it," I
said. "I shall make a legal challenge to the Prime
Minister of Canada to preserve the right to read
books untaxed."

Famous writers applauded me.

"But I will need your support," I continued,
feeling like a politician myself.

They hooted with self-conscious restraint,
then left, driving back to Toronto in their long,

sleek cars. They said they wanted to give me time to work, yet in their mass departure I saw a rehearsal of the abandonment I would face if my enterprise failed.

As I read about the history of the Canadian Senate as the peaceful domain of the sober second thought, my anger grew. Not only was reading being assailed by this wanton enlargement; a kind of aristocracy was being threatened with destruction. Canadianness—the Canadianness I loved and embraced—was rooted in sedate aristocracy: my apartment above the mill-run, the nineteenth-century architecture of my village, the invitations to boards and broadcasts that enabled me to earn a living without slaving as other lawyers slaved. Like Milly's friends, I felt the prime minister's manipulations as a personal attack.

My anger swelled as I wrote my brief. I made a plea for freedom of speech, freedom of access to culture rather than, as I asserted would be the outcome of the prime minister's tax on books, freedom from culture. During long nights fuelled by strong black tea, a dash of potent feeling—was this loyalty to my new country or devotion to Milly?—coalesced into pages of prose, a firm entity that had not been there before. As I reread my text, I marvelled at the artful use of precedent, the passion and conviction, and the grasp of constitutional history that resounded in my document. I stumbled to bed, deciding to mail in my challenge in the morning.

After that, everything happened fast. I received a confirmation by telegram, then a phone call from Milly. "Come over here," she said. "They're debating the new tax." When I arrived at her house, she was in the living room with a bottle of Cabernet Sauvignon. The fountain in the yard had been turned off, her husband was away, the lights were dimmed. We awaited the evening news. She motioned me to sit on the couch and sat down beside me. She wore a long, august, vice-presidential dress, which flipped up when she crossed her right leg over her left, revealing pale flesh. She plied me with wine. "What you've done is wonderful, R. U. You're a wonderful man. Our friends will be so proud of us. There's no doubting that we belong." As the final words slipped out, her expression shifted from effusive to ironic. After the second glass of wine, the warmth flowed back. She leaned against me. I was ebullient with achievement, and eager for the delights that awaited me in my future.

My heart—but only my heart—rose to meet Milly's flesh.

She gave me a leering smile. Her arrogance was a form of teasing, even affection. A homage to our collaboration, that smile sealed our intimacy. Her grandfather clock struck ten. Milly clicked the remote control to turn on the CBC. The voice of Knowlton Nash filled the room, reading the day's news. "Today the prime minister found himself facing fresh challenges to his plan to enlarge the Senate, including a legal challenge!"

Reclined on the chesterfield, our heads side by side, we watched the nation consecrate the scheming of two fugitive foreigners. The screen displayed a scene from that afternoon, the sun shining down on Ottawa. The prime minister strode out of Parliament. Reporters hurled questions at him. One of the reporters, in a voice that made my heart clench, asked him about the legal challenge to his actions launched by "the southwestern Ontario lawyer, R. U. Singh."

The prime minister snapped upright, as though a rod had been driven up his spine. Wielding his jaw like a weapon, he stepped towards the crowd. "I've never heard of Mr. Singh!" he snarled. Surrounded by aides and Mounties, he pushed past the scrum.

"R. U.! You're famous!"

Milly grabbed my head, as though plucking an artifact off a shelf. She kissed me hard on the cheek and slithered to her feet, the drooping wings of her dress exposing her legs. "Get out of here!"

"Pardon me?"

"You're famous. Your phone will be ringing. You must be at home to answer it. The rest of your life depends on it!"

I straightened my turban and headed for the door. As I walked downhill towards the river, every shop was closed. They were all at home watching the CBC. They had heard my name on television. I had never been so widely known, so accompanied in my new country. It felt thrilling to be alone on the street, passing under tall lamps that illumined venerable red brick and washed-out limestone in silence so deep that I could hear the burbling of the river at the bottom of the hill. As I descended the slope, I felt myself going up and down at the same time: my body dropping towards the river as morsels of my being levitated into warm night air shot through with televised ether. R. U. Singh, the southwestern Ontario lawyer, diffused across Canada: I straddled the nation, drenching it in my essence.

NINE
great expectations

When I came in the door of my flat, the red stud of my answering machine was flashing. I pressed the button: *You have eleven new messages.* As I reached to play them, the phone rang. It was a journalist who wanted to know why I had used the word "stacking" in my brief: wasn't it particularly harsh to say that the Prime Minister was "stacking" the Senate? Did I have prior political affiliations? Was I connected to the Official Opposition? "By instinct," I replied, "I am an aristocrat and a conservative. And I am a proud Canadian citizen. Citizenship has its responsibilities. One of them is to preserve democracy."

How they adored that line! "An aristocrat of democracy": I repeated the words twenty times that night, and thirty times the next day. I belaboured my adopted colony-nation with its Victorian heritage of aristocratic democracy. Before I could finish my breakfast, I was a model New Canadian, a budding member of the country's enshrined hierarchy of chatterers. I was waiting for my coffee to boil when the girl from the bakery came to my door, waving that morning's *Globe and Mail*. Fetching in her blue jeans and ponytail, she told me her father sent me the paper with his compliments. Near the bottom of the front page was my law-school graduation photograph! I was astonished that they had found it.

By noon, men with bulky cameras were at my door. I posed with the rapids in the background while my neighbours stared. A professor from Milly's university who lived in the village, and was fond of parading along the river in sandals and socks, greeted me as though we were comrades. Knowing he hated my Milly, I gauged his hypocrisy with a cold eye. The men with cameras elbowed him aside. Excitement combed through me until I became addicted to it. I sat in my flat, waiting for the phone to ring. If half an hour passed without a call I felt neglected. I lived for each fresh interview, each acknowledgement that

I was an object of spectacle. I stopped reading. I watched every newscast my television could receive, waiting for references to myself. Interviewed on television, I remained calm and factual, a source of serene wisdom and moral probity.

After the first interview aired, a fresh gale of phone calls blew through my flat. Law-school classmates sent congratulatory notes on letterhead stationery. Esther phoned to say that she was proud of me. Even Shelley (or was it Melissa?) found my number and offered me effusive congratulations.

With time, the requests for interviews tapered off. Fickle journalists turned their attention elsewhere. Another sort of phone call, less frequent yet more significant, came to the fore. I heard from a community college in suburban Toronto where eighty-five per cent of the students were immigrants or the children of immigrants. They offered me a healthy fee to speak about immigrants in Canadian society. A newspaper asked for a column, and also offered a fee. The organizers of a class-action suit invited me to join their legal team.

By the end of the week, I had more work than I could ever complete. My head was in a whirl.

I was a man of standing in my new country, but I had lost my squire's leisure. Gone were my evenings immersed in Trollope or Thomas Hardy, my afternoon teas by the water with Milly. The hike up the street to her house was an excursion I would need to schedule for the scarce spare moments permitted by our respective agendas.

Every day I seemed to be driving into Toronto, and when I came home late at night, or the next morning, after a night with Chyou, my answering machine was pulsing. I saw Milly and her friends less often, and when I did, we met not in their garden, but at events in Toronto at which literature or human rights—or, as was often the case, both—were celebrated. I wore a tuxedo and a turban. The men gave me hearty handshakes and cuffed me on the shoulder as though I were a boon companion; the women delivered dry kisses to my cheek. They looked at me with relief, confirming my impression, formed on the afternoon I had entered Milly's garden, that they lived in a world where they did not meet people whom they did not already know. I had become one of the people whom they knew. I was a brown-skinned bearded man in a turban for whose rise into the Canadian spotlight they would take credit.

They slapped my back or kissed my cheek with the same stiff-bodied restraint they expressed with their white Ontarian compatriots. Respect tempered their familiarity; they asked me to comment on the outlook in my "community," by which they meant Indians, South Asians, all Asians, all people of colour. Constricted by this multi-purpose role, I was noncommittal in my replies. I avoided provoking activist hotheads, I did not pretend to be a spokesman for the people in the towers, whom I was pleased to have put behind me. Following my mentors' example, I sat on the moderate liberal fence. I was as harmless and ineffectual as a Canadian writer, committing myself to campaigns that failed as activism yet succeeded as public relations.

My legal challenge to the prime minister's enlargement of the Senate bogged down in court. The government's lawyers issued procedural objection after procedural objection, repelling all discussion of the case's substance until it was too late. The enlarged Senate, with a majority that supported the prime minister, introduced the tax on books. Milly's friends moved on, their books selling as well as ever, and found fresh outrages to denounce. My challenge had inflicted little damage on the prime minister—though the word "stacking" crept into news reports—but it continued to benefit me. Each time the government issued another procedural objection, I was interviewed on radio and television, and after each round of interviews, I received offers to speak, write, or represent new clients.

I mitigated the onrush of fame by reminding myself of the reserve and discretion commended by the novels I read. I tried to be as discreet as a Jane Austen matron, as opaque as a Henry James narrator. Though my turban had become my visual signature, I obviated explicit associations with Sikhdom. Canadians prized authenticity: I must not violate their values by risking exposure as a non-Sikh. I declined offers to talk about Sikh politics, or participate on panels with Sikh community leaders. I was in my element as the representative Indian in radio or television debates in which the other panel members were not Indian. When, in the midst of my legal challenge to the prime minister, the woman of iron who ruled India was assassinated, I commented in general terms on the years of her government, passing over the fact that she had been murdered by her Sikh bodyguards in retaliation for her attack on the Golden Temple. (The left-armed fast bowler, raging over the phone about Sikh secessionism, served notice that Hindus in India no longer regarded Sikhs with the equanimity my father had shown.) The next summer, when an Air India flight blew up over Ireland, I refrained from entering into discussions of Sikh politics, limiting myself to reprimanding the prime minister for having responded to the disaster by sending a letter of condolence to the government of India when more than three quarters of the dead were Canadians like myself. Each interview I did on this subject consolidated my Canadianness.

Money was no longer a problem, except in the sense that my means exceeded my needs. I had to decide whether to continue to let a flat, or to buy a house like Milly's; whether to trade in the aging second-hand compact car for a new vehicle; whether to invest my money or to spend it. When I met the bearded swashbuckler or the woman with the gravel voice, circumspection muted their greetings. I took their guardedness as a compliment, reading in it a recognition that I had developed my own circle of influence. There were the CBC panels where I appeared, my weekly opinion piece on multicultural television,

a newspaper chain where I was a monthly colum-
nist. Beyond these activities, which belonged to a
world that the writers understood, was my legal
work, which they did not understand, but which
they knew earned me an income.

With success came notoriety in my own *community*. I learned that I was not the only Indian in
southwestern Ontario. There were others in London and Kitchener-Waterloo, and even in smaller
outposts. It became a matter of prestige for these
people to engage me to represent them. I was del-
uged with requests for work from Indians who
were buying condominiums, Indians who were
writing wills, Indians who were separating from
the Indian spouses with whom they had immigrated in order to wrap their arms around white
Canadian bodies. These transactions—bit work,
in most cases, that paid no more than a few hundred dollars—became so numerous that I sometimes lost track of them. Caught up in my hectic
travel agenda, I forgot to finish them on time and
had to be reminded with letters and phone calls. I
came home from Toronto (or, after my columns
on immigrant issues became syndicated, from Ottawa, Montreal, Halifax, Calgary, or Vancouver)
to be surprised by impatient Indian voices on my

answering machine. This was more of a home-coming than I desired. It was like being back in Bombay, and not in a way that pleased me. This hectoring on the part of my clients, far from being efficacious, often had the reverse effect, making me dawdle even more in my legal work as I threw my energy into the world of newspapers, radio, and television: into activities that gained me public notice, reminding Milly of my existence. Each time my name was broadcast in public, I wondered whether Milly would catch wind of it and invite me to come and see her.

One evening, when I had just driven back from an event in Hamilton, the phone rang, and the Indian voice I heard belonged to my cousin. He reminded me that he had looked after me when I arrived on the Greyhound bus from Thunder Bay; that he had sublet me rooms in his apartments for nearly a decade.

"I am fed up with paying rent, R. U. I am fed up with being so far out. Can't you buy me something downtown? A good place to live? Your brother says you're richer than he is now. Don't forget who gave you your start, you ungrateful sister-sleeper—"

I cursed my eldest brother. My cousin did not

read Canadian newspapers or watch Canadian television—not even multicultural television—and would have remained oblivious to my success had the left-armed fast bowler not boasted about me. I squirmed to get this hanger-on off the phone. He failed to realize that the man he was talking to did not exist. In truth, neither of the men to whom he might have been speaking could be said to exist: neither the morose, introverted fellow in the Toronto Maple Leafs baseball cap who had slouched through humiliating jobs and with whom he had shared dowdy apartments, nor "the southwestern Ontario lawyer R. U. Singh," a person about whom my cousin knew nothing other than that he had money. The first fellow had long since disappeared, and, as for the second, not even I was properly acquainted with him. Late at night, turning on the television—I now had the full range of cable channels—I would watch "R. U. Singh" discoursing on subjects of which I had only the most superficial knowledge. I marvelled at his self-confidence, his firm, grey-whiskered presence on the screen, his unflappable calm.

If, during my years in Toronto, my being had been muffled by drudgery, success, by contrast, had pulled me out of myself. A few of my salient characteristics—not always, I felt, the most important ones—had been sucked out, baked solid beneath the kiln of television lights, and exposed in public like a death mask. Sometimes I opened the newspaper and read that the signatories to a petition included the southwestern Ontario lawyer R. U. Singh, or that R. U. Singh, the noted commentator on ethnic relations, had made a declaration about immigration or integration or racism. I would hesitate, failing to connect that enterprising fellow with myself. The words that Singh sang felt disconnected from my soul. Before his certainties, my perceptions dissolved into inchoate clouds, fleeing the steady march of raptly structured sentences that flowed from the composed fellow on the screen as he articulated worthy sentiments, some variant of which someone else had always expressed before him.

Fame may not be an aphrodisiac, but it allows one to meet people. For nearly ten years I had spoken only to my cousin, his friends, their relatives, and a succession of surly employers. Now I met new people, many of them charming and intelligent, every week. When one is introduced as an important person, women linger at one's side over a second drink. I do not wish to sound like a Casanova, and I have not been one, but I will admit that, in addition to Chyou, who continued to receive my visits, other opportunities presented themselves. Not in all cases did I reject them. Most of these events—now that I was older, the word *tryst* sounded too risqué—occurred in hotel rooms after dinners or conferences. They had little life beyond the moment that brought the bodies together, though they certainly made my life more exciting. Since I could not tell Chyou about these adventures—our relationship was not quite that open—I recounted them to Milly. They became part of our mutual titillation, the currency of our salacious friendship, as we raised the stakes by proving to ourselves just how frank we could be with each other. As we each became more successful, we saw each other less and less. The fact that we did not speak often challenged us to be more daring, more open, on the rare occasions when we had time to talk, as though this would reconfirm our essential bond.

One evening, when I had no events and no pending legal work beyond the separation agreements of disenchanted Indians, I left my flat, where I continued to live because I did not have time to buy a house. I walked up the street, as I had on my first afternoon in the village. I was planning a trip to Asia to spend some of the money I had made, to demonstrate to my family that the fifth son was not the failure they had expected, and to pay my respects to my father in his declining years. When I reached Milly's house, the fountain was silent and the lights were off. I rang the doorbell. Her husband answered. His hair was long and completely white. Looking down from his teetering American height, he said that Milly was away. "She's always away these days." His jowls were inert, like those of a hunting dog in repose.

The dynamics of Milly's marriage had reversed. Isolated from his readers in the Deep South, her husband had seen his audience shrivel. His wilder-than-Faulkner extravagance was off-putting to cautious Canadians. Fewer and fewer invitations to travel, read, and seduce younger women now came his way. Milly, by contrast, was in demand. She was travelling often and—though she was more discreet with me than I was with her—it was now she who had adventures.

"She goes to conferences on *ac-a-dem-ic ad-min-i-stra-tion*," her husband said in the slow tones that I had learned to refer to as a drawl. "I used to get invited to read at shindigs like that. Now they all want Milly." I realized that he had been sampling the house's stock of wine. "Milly's planning her next move. I bet you it's gonna be a big one."

"That will be good for you," I said, hoping I sounded polite.

"Yup. I guess I'll be along for the ride."

Imagining that he was trying to decide whether to invite me in, I spared us both this discomfort. Asking him to give Milly my regards, I left.

TEN
vanity fair

Two weeks later, I saw her.

The conference was in Montreal. As we were speaking on different panels, I had not been aware that she would be there. Having spotted her name on the program, I attended her event. She came on stage dressed in white like an apparition: white slacks, white jacket, a cream-coloured blouse. She was trim and looked younger than her age. Her hair was as voluminous as ever, and just as blond. As I listened to her speak, I marvelled at how she had expunged the Deep South from her voice. Unlike her husband, Milly sounded as though she had been born in Canada. She had advanced as a chameleon, while I was a more boldly sketched portrait of the man I might have been at home had I been a first son rather than a fifth, or had I been born a generation earlier, when the need to earn money was less urgent and one could comport oneself as a squire. My sole true charade, an outrageous one, lay in my masquerading as a Sikh. Yet in our own ways, each of us was in disguise.

After Milly's panel had ended, I waited on the edge of the crowd. She noticed me. I imagined I saw the corner of her mouth jut up in mid-sentence. She patted a man in a navy blue jacket on the shoulder to dismiss him, then turned towards me. "R. U.! I was hoping I'd see you here!" We hugged. The kisses she gave me on both cheeks had nothing of the dry peck of Ontario. Our effusiveness dispatched those who were lingering with questions. We glanced into each other's eyes to confirm that our bond remained potent. "Let's get out of here," Milly said.

I followed her out of the conference hotel and into the street. The smell of French fries saturated the cold air. The dim pavement in front of us receded into darkness. I glimpsed the silhouette of Mount Royal squeezed between two office towers. Milly looped her arm in mine. We promenaded like a courting couple. "This used to be the red-light district," Milly said, gesturing at rashes of garish neon.

Women whose stockings were held up by suspenders loitered in doorways. My failed French course at Lakehead University allowed me to read that on this corner, "tourist rooms" were rented by the hour. A breeze of a chill unexpected in June penetrated my spine. "Let's find somewhere to go," Milly said. "I've got things to tell you."

She directed me towards a derelict building on the south side of the street that looked as though it had once been the private home of a moneyed family. We were in a district with snack bars that offered *frites* and *poutine*, dark doorways of clubs that promised *XXX* videos, shuttered Vietnamese pho houses, and striding ruffians with unkempt moustaches and tattooed necks. The wooden mansion, whose balconies, jutting at odd angles, interrupted the regular progression of its four storeys, resembled a ship from a more stately era that had set out on a journey of exploration and run aground in the grim present. I was startled when Milly turned towards the door. Mentioning the name of a well-known gay writer, she said he had assured her it was worth the visit, and that everyone was welcome.

There was no security guard; no one asked us

to pay a cover charge. We walked down a long corridor in which the light had a purple tint and menacing music played. I felt as though I had entered a dimension where the boundaries of my being expanded and contracted in unforeseen directions. The mansion's rooms were in near-darkness. There were extravagant chandeliers and a plethora of leather couches on which men were embracing men. This sight startled me less than the mansion's emptiness. By the time we reached the second floor, we were nearly alone. The threatening music trembled through rough, unvarnished floorboards. On the third storey the corridor opened onto the stage of a small theatre. We looked down, captured in our performance: the stalls were nearly empty. Two slender young men sat in the front row.

"No way that beard is real," one of them said.

We hurried off the stage and emerged into a room that opened onto one of the mansion's balconies. Here there was a bar and tables; tinny, rhythmic music was playing. Milly suggested we sit down. A waiter appeared. We each ordered a glass of Pinot Grigio. "To commemorate our first glass of wine together," I said.

Milly's announcement that she had news had

made me nervous even before we had ventured into this disorienting building. I laid my hands close to hers on the table, then withdrew them, fearing that in this environment it might be unseemly for a man to touch a woman's hand.

"You can hold my hand if you like," Milly said. "They think you're a woman in drag."

"My family thought I came to Canada because I was that sort of man. That is my news: I am going to make a trip home. My brothers know now that I am a man of the world ..."

"So it's safe for you to go back without a wife in tow. So much the better for you, R. U. Spouses can be a pain in the ass. It would be much easier if we could make them appear when we need them and disappear when we don't."

She raised her glass; we clinked. "Cheers, R. U. You and I have brought each other good luck." Without awaiting my affirmation, she went on. "I'm going to ask you a favour. I'll pay you for it, but it's still a favour because I want it to be done by you and only you. I'm going to need utter, absolute, fucking discretion."

"Milly ..."

"I want you to prepare a separation agreement for me."

"From your husband?"

"Is there anyone else I can be separated from? Not from you, that's for sure. You and I will always be buddies, R. U. But I've reached a stage where I need to get him out of my hair."

"You've been through so much together."

She leaned forward, modulating her voice as meticulously as she had an hour earlier during the panel discussion. "R. U., I've had an interview for a job as president of a university. A second interview. I can't tell you the name of the university, but you can see that this is a once-in-a-lifetime opportunity."

I remembered her husband's prediction that Milly's next move would be a big one. Did he suspect her plan to leave him? "Congratulations, Milly. I can't think of anyone who deserves it more. But why can't your husband accompany you? I'm sure he'd be pleased to—"

"He's always pleased to have me support him. But I can't afford him any more."

"Is his drinking so expensive?"

She smiled. "His talking costs me more than his drinking. R. U., my husband isn't like you and me. He's more like that cousin of yours. He doesn't want to integrate into Canada; he just wants to sit around thinking about where he was reared and writing stories about it. I am about"—she raised crossed fingers— "to become the president of a Canadian university. I am being hired from my present university on the assumption that I am a Canadian with years of experience in the Canadian university system. Every time my husband opens his mouth, he exposes me as a foreigner. We've been here for more than twenty years and he still sounds like he's walked off the set of *The Beverly Hillbillies*! It hasn't mattered much until now because we haven't been living and working in the same town. Most of my colleagues at the university have never met my husband. They know he's a writer, and that's fine. They don't have to deal with him. They don't have the Deep South thrown in their faces every time he opens his mouth. It won't be like that when I become a president. A university president has an official residence close to campus. She hosts dinner parties at which everybody has a drink yet no one drinks to excess."

Against my will, I wanted to defend the husband. Milly's urge to cut him loose was an upheaval I wished to quash. This sort of instability put my connection to her, also, at risk. "I'm sure he'll learn—"

"I'm sure he won't." The tinny music made Milly's ferocity twice as frightening. A willowy waiter ducked through the darkness and asked us in French if we wanted another drink. I hadn't noticed that our glasses were empty. "*Oui. Encore une fois*," Milly said to the waiter. When he returned with our second round, she resumed in a less challenging voice. "R. U., imagine if you had come here with a traditional Indian wife from Bombay. Imagine what a burden she would be in your present life."

I tried to imagine this. It was nearly unimaginable. Certainly the thought was unpalatable. Seizing on my hesitation, Milly continued: "I cannot afford to have my husband getting drunk, I can't afford to have him reminding everyone that I'm an American every time he opens his mouth, and I especially can't afford to have him seducing undergraduate women at a university of which I'm president." She let this sink in. "Believe me, all of those things will happen. Unless my dear friend R. U. draws up a separation agreement for me."

"A separation agreement," I said, "is an agreement. Both wife and husband contribute to the conditions."

"Well, I'm very sorry, but my husband isn't

going to get that chance. Since he doesn't have an income, he doesn't have any leverage. As soon as the job's confirmed, I'm presenting him with a *fait accompli*. He will receive a small income from my salary as payment for not coming with me. He can go back down home or he can stay in Canada."

"Stay in the village," I murmured.

"No. The house in the village will be sold."

"Oh, Milly."

I was terribly sad. It was the end of an era that had brought me most of what I had wanted in life. I mourned the lustre the village would lose with Milly's departure. I would roam the vacant streets like Marcel bereft in a Paris abandoned by the Duchess of Guermantes. My brilliant hostess would be far away. I would never again hear the fountain tinkling in Milly's garden, or, if I did, other, coarser people would be sitting at the long oak table: not artists concerned about the fate of the world, but ordinary louts who swilled beer and talked about American football. How could I be a country squire without a country society at the level to which I aspired?

"We'll still be friends, won't we?"

"We'll be better friends than ever, R. U. The higher you and your friends climb, the more vital your loyalty to each other becomes." She sipped her drink. A pair of very tall women sat down at the table next to us. They glanced in our direction from beneath thick false eyelashes. One of them pointed at my turban and said something in French.

"Once I'm a university president, I'll have a certain pull. For example, I'll be able to nominate people for the Order of Canada."

"You will appear particularly enlightened if you nominate someone who is a visible minority." I lifted her hand to my lips. The wine had gone to my head. I imagined myself being introduced on television as a Member of the Order of Canada, a man who had risen from distributing flyers to automobile windshields to shaking the hand of the Governor General. Few distinctions could do more to confirm my aristocracy and consecrate me as the public representative of Canada's ethnic communities.

"It will be good for both of us. And I'll do it, I promise you I will, R. U. As long as you have my separation agreement ready the second I get the phone call confirming that I have the job."

I returned her hand to the table, imagining myself alone in the village, the fountain silenced. In compensation I would have a new sign hanging at the bottom of my staircase: R. U. *Singh, Attorney at Law. B.A., M.A., LL.B., Q.C., O.C.* I closed my eyes. The final two letters would be concrete testimony that I had joined the upper echelons of people who mattered. How many immigrants had attained such heights?

"It will be a pleasure to write your separation agreement, Milly."

"Good. I'll send you a list of the conditions I want included. You can write them up in legalese." An anxious look pinched her face. In these moments of overt calculation, when the skin around her eyes wrinkled, she looked her age. "Do you think you can do it before you leave for India?"

"Of course."

What would I not do for my Milly?

ELEVEN
bleak house

The next evening I returned to the village. When I woke in the morning to the gurgling of the rapids, I went downstairs and found a letter that had been mailed express sticking out from the ruck of morning mail. Milly, as always, was efficient. I opened the envelope and surveyed the points she wanted included. If he signed this agreement, her husband would receive a basic income that Milly reserved the right to terminate if he came within twenty-five kilometres of the city where she was working, or if he discussed her or their marriage in comments that were recorded on radio, television, or film, or were printed in a book, magazine, or newspaper.

I sat down at my desk. I turned on the computer

I had started to use for legal work a few years earlier. I began to cut and paste the set phrases of separation agreements, arrange them on the screen, and enter the details that Milly had given me. My stomach churned. The clauses I was editing made me ill. I was dismantling the foundations of my life, divorcing myself from my own existence. But I could not refuse Milly this favour. Even if she had not dangled the Order of Canada before my eyes, I would have provided this service with the enthusiasm of her most loyal servant—and, naturally, without sending her a bill.

Milly and I would always be in drag together: migrant fugitives dressed up to blend in, sharing the secrets of each other's disguises. Yet she was so much more effortless and elegant than I, so much more ruthless, behind the smile she never allowed to falter, so much better at passing for a Canadian. I would never cease to worship and be intimidated by her. If she left, if she ceased to be securely bound in her marriage, the tensions that held us together in a force field in which we were never truly apart yet never became too close for comfort, in which titillation was eternal and jealousy was unknown, would rupture, spilling us apart like apples rolling off in opposite directions, getting bruised and battered on the way.

As the morning light climbed higher, casting shadows over the far side of the ravine through which the rapids ran, I saw that the dissolution of Milly's marriage would explode the triangular tensions that held us together. I was not worried that she would fail to carry through on her promise of an Order of Canada. As I stared with a blank gaze at the screen of my computer, my malaise ran deeper. As a single woman, Milly would have no husband to bore and exasperate her, or to drive her to take refuge in my company. She might have affairs: precisely targeted affairs, I was certain, that would weld passion to ambition. These events would displace our tender understanding, our perfect, unending, never-to-be-consummated-yet-never-to-be-broken dalliance of mind and soul. I did not want her marriage, our marriage, to end. I did not want her to leave the village.

I could not refuse to write this agreement. And I could not write it.

I paced my room. I dragged my suitcase out of the closet and began to pack for my trip. I packed only clothes and a few books. I refused to play the role of the munificent Western relative, in which I had seen my cousin's friends and their wives indulge by returning to India with boxes of unaffordable electronic baubles intended not to delight relatives at home, but rather to dazzle them with the giver's foreign-gained wealth. The givers then spent most of the year paying off their aggressive generosity. Though better off than any of them, I was returning home on a register of restraint. I planned to be remote, dignified, and moderate.

I told myself that Milly was my friend, that I should do this promptly, as she had asked, and send it to her office at the university by registered mail. Yet as I sat down, driving myself on with this motto of obligation, I was stymied. My fingers typed nonsense full of spelling mistakes. I could not bear to see the standard clauses that I had saved on my computer punctuated by the name "Millicent Crowe." Unwanted, a memory surfaced of a conversation I'd had with that disagreeable professor who lived in the village. He had told me that among the university faculty Milly was known as "Militant Cow." I caught myself typing the words "Militant Cow" in place of my dear Milly's name. I deleted the error and laid my head down on my desk. I turned off my computer, went out for a stroll along the water as far as the old mill that was being converted into condominiums, and stared into the turbulence of rapids and tiny black-water whirlpools. I went home, turned on the computer, then got up to continue packing. By evening my suitcase was nearly ready. But Milly's separation agreement remained uncompleted.

I left for home. Or so, imitating the diction of my cousin and his friends, of S. A. Singh up in Thunder Bay, I insisted on thinking of India. I knew that now my home was a southwestern Ontario village, or a Toronto television studio; yet, lapsing into an impulse that I reprimanded in other immigrants, I fed myself the myth of an idyllic place of ancestral origin. That old place would spare me from the travails of the present. Except, as I would discover over the next three weeks, I was not going home. I was going to a country which, like the country I had grown up in, was called "India." There the resemblance ended. The India I visited had been purged of the phantoms of Rudyard Kipling; no one dreamed of being a country squire. Buildings I remembered had been demolished, the smog was impenetrable, everyone spoke on cellphones, the electronic toys my cousin took home in triumph were available in every shopping centre, and even gentle Hindus had become fundamentalists. Everyone spoke of prosperity, yet I saw only the fraying of an ancient culture. And the traffic! It made me vow to never again complain about the 401.

I was received as an object of curiosity. Unable to perpetrate the charade of being a Sikh on my native soil, I had left my turban in the village. My beard had been trimmed to a close-cropped greyish fuzz, and my hair cut to just below my ears. I looked like an Indian mimicking Western bohemianism, a Dickensian gentleman dyed brown. As I observed myself in the mirror of the plane's toilet on the flight from Toronto to Hong Kong, I realized that this was the role it fell to me to play. I must satisfy the belief that I was returning in triumph from a world that my family could not hope to understand. I stopped off for a few days each in Hong Kong and Singapore, then went on to Bombay. Even the city's name was about to change. In order to extirpate the colonial heritage that was my most cherished tie with the place, Bombay was going to be renamed Mumbai. My horror at this decision made me an object of ridicule. Even the left-armed fast bowler, a compendium of reactionary opinions, regarded the change of name as progress. My days in Hong Kong and Singapore enabled me to understand this changed India as part of a continuum of Asian success.

To my frustration, rather than being awed by me, my family found me quaint. "Are you my son?" my father said, crumpled in the garden chair where he spent his days attended by servants. "You look like a man from my parents' generation. I would expect you to be my granduncle, not my child."

"I take that as a compliment, Father."

I was less demure when my nephews and nieces found me old-fashioned. At the very least, I would have expected them to confront a paradox in the sight of a man who had returned from the First World steeped in traditional learning. But, to my astonishment, my quaintness fulfilled the young people's expectations. It corroborated their view of North America as yesterday's modernity, one step behind their own.

I took notes on their comments, thinking of columns I would write when I returned. This was the only time that thoughts of Milly entered my head. I remembered the unfinished separation agreement and told myself that Milly would not mind, and that I would complete it as soon as I got home. Because, I was now certain, a colonial village in southwestern Ontario was my home.

When I returned, my mailbox was full of imperious-looking letters and telegrams. Ignoring them, I went to sleep. In the morning I bound my head in my turban, feeling like myself for the first time in three weeks. I left for Toronto, where I was due to make a television appearance. The lights of the CBC studio on Front Street were hot. The gasping, humid heat of India had depleted me, but this familiar baking invigorated me. My home and native land was not simply Canada; it was the Canadian mediascape: this was my habitat.

I revelled in my panel discussion, illustrating my points with examples from my recent trip. I was a worldly, well-travelled fellow, a cosmopolitan authority in addition to being a native informant from one of our land's multicultural communities. Recalling the sensation of being seen as a man in drag with Milly in the mansion in Montreal, I felt reconciled with myself. I was myself, and I was also "R. U. Singh," who incarnated multiculturalism on television. My journey to the home that was no longer mine had laid to rest my unease at the thought that my core reposed in a phantom of the airwaves. As I shook hands with the host and my fellow panellists at the end of the taping, I knew that from now on I would enjoy my accidental occidental career as never before.

I was on my way out of the CBC building, walking through the glass atrium, when a reporter I'd met once before, a rough-edged fellow who wore baggy suits and covered Ontario politics, flagged me down. "What's this I hear about the Law Society investigating you? What's going on?"

"No one is investigating me," I said, more amused than startled. "Who told you that?"

"I'm told there's a deposition."

"Rumours started by friends of our former prime minister, I suspect." I mustered my most urbane smile. I clapped him on the shoulder. We shared a laugh.

I retrieved my car from the underground parking lot, then crawled through snarled traffic all the way to the Gardiner Expressway, where I entered hordes of swerving, demented drivers. I was well outside Toronto before I had time to reflect on my encounter in the atrium. I acknowledged a certain unease. My law practice had provided me with steady work after my confrontation with the prime minister. Having no place for a secretary in my flat, I had continued to keep track of my correspondence myself, which meant I did not keep track of it well. An accountant down the street straightened out my finances at the end of the year, but I had no one to file my letters. I opened letters when I had time, choosing those whose return addresses indicated that they were connected with matters that were on my mind, or those that looked as though they contained a cheque, or a promising invitation. The others piled up on my desk. The pile, to be honest, was voluminous. Most of it was junk mail, but I supposed it was possible that I might have missed something important.

When I returned to the village, welcomed by its venerable limestone and the chattering of the rapids, I found a fresh harvest of envelopes in my mailbox. Though residual jetlag was creeping back, draining away the exhilaration of my television appearance, I took the cardboard box where I had been storing correspondence for weeks and turned it upside down on my kitchen table. I rifled through the pile, looking for envelopes from the Law Society of Upper Canada. I had taken these to be service bulletins or reminders of membership dues. I opened them. The printed words shocked me. A man at home in his books, I knew that printed words were truth: this truth rebuked me. I felt as though my very existence had been impugned. Weeks ago, a certain Gita Kidambi had filed a complaint against me, alleging that she had paid me $3,000.00 to draw up a marital separation agreement (I vaguely recalled her visit: a thin Tamil woman who lived in Kitchener). She further alleged that I had cashed her cheque (this was possible) and that I had done no work on her file (this, I admitted, was all too likely). Ms. Kidambi asserted that she was unemployed and needed the separation agreement to oblige her husband to support her while she looked for work.

My shock receded once I had finished reading the letter. This was a matter that I could dispatch with a couple of phone calls. When I rang the Law Society, I got the answering machine. I paced the kitchen, then staged a fresh assault on the mail. I was rewarded with the discovery of a cheque for a television appearance I had forgotten. Beneath this envelope were others from the Law Society. *Since we have not received a reply to our notice of May 10, we ask that you give these allegations*

118

*all due attention … * Then: *As you have failed to reply to repeated communications, we have no alternative but to refer this matter to a disciplinary panel. This panel is comprised of two lawyers and one lay bencher …*

My breath shortened. I resumed pacing. I told myself to be calm. Still dehydrated from the plane, I drank water from the tap, eschewing the Cabernet Sauvignon I had promised myself to celebrate my television appearance. I had to attend to this mess instantly. If the disciplinary panel had met already, I might have no choice but to ask for a suspension of my right to practise law while I drew up Ms. Kidambi's separation agreement.

I continued opening letters. The shock, the kick in the stomach, from which I have not recovered to this day, came in the next letter. A second complaint had been added to the first. This complaint was from Professor Millicent Crowe, B.A., M.A., Ph.D., D.LITT., F.R.S.C., O.C., President of the University of South Saskatchewan. Like Ms. Kidambi, Professor Crowe alleged that I had failed to complete a separation agreement for which she had contracted me.

My Milly! My dearest friend, my eternal flame, with whom my bond was sweeter than that of any lover because it was untainted by the disappointments of intimacy, the daily griping of cohabitation, the beady-eyed knowingness of those whose bodies have coupled. What a terrible misunderstanding!

I lifted the receiver and rang her number. There was no reply. I left the kitchen and went out the door. Day was turning into night, summer into autumn; the rapids hissed over the rocks as the water level dropped at the end of the season. I clumped down the stairs, walked past the river-front shops and cafés, then turned up the hill, as I had on my first visit to the village. Without my bold step into the garden that day, I would not have become a man of substance. Longing coursed through me for my literary loitering, for bright afternoons of fine wines and a splashing fountain in the company of famous scribblers; yet the memories only heightened my alarm. What had gone wrong? My Milly could not have done this to me. The complaint to the Law Society must be the result of academic politics, of some scheme to discredit her in her new job.

Who knew what forces were conspiring against us?

I reached the house to find a sign with the red-and-white logo of a real-estate company planted on the front lawn. Taped over the discreet *For Sale* sign was a bright red *Sold*. Had Milly completed her move from the village during my August vacation? I knocked on the door again and again, hoping to commiserate with her husband, hoping he might tell me how to contact the woman we both adored. There was no one. I stepped into the garden, as I had that first afternoon. The lawn was empty, the fountain extinguished. The long oak table, the core of our conviviality, had been carted away, leaving an indented nub of flattened yellow grass where each leg had stood. The flowers were in bloom. The care to which the yard had been subjected accentuated its vacancy. Drained of humanity, it was a museum.

I left the garden and stood in front of the house. I must talk to her.

"Hey, R. U. Did Militant Cow fuck you over and leave? What did you expect? Militant makes and Militant breaks."

I feared these words had surged up from the ugliest corner of my psyche. I trembled at the thought that such mutinous hatred lurked inside my purest feelings. It was a relief to turn and find the professor, unshaven for the summer, his greying curls in need of a trim, walking his dog along the street.

"Has she left already?" I asked.

"Left us, and left you in the lurch." He shuffled his Birkenstocks; a toe poked through a hole in his left sock. His dog, a prissy poodle, sniffed the grass as if in disdain. "Nobody at the university's shedding any tears. But you shouldn't have dragged your feet on her separation agreement, R. U. You caused her tons of grief. Her hubby tried to go out west for the ride. She finally got rid of him, but it was ugly. He showed up drunk at her official residence. Her first act as prez was to call the campus cops to haul him away." He pulled on his dog's leash. "Nobody does that to Militant Cow and gets away with it."

"We are friends. Fellow immigrants."

"I hate to tell you, R. U., but you are a visible minority. When the going gets tough, those nice multicultural sentiments you talk about on TV aren't worth squat. Especially if you go up against a white woman from the empire next door. Militant being militant, she'll make sure you get screwed up the ass in public."

"This is wrong." I remembered the facile formulae of my professors in Thunder Bay. This man was no different; he was as superficial as they, and just as wrong. "Milly and I are fugitives together."

"It's your funeral."

He shrugged his shoulders and swung the poodle's leash as though he were redirecting a horse. He left me alone in the dusk. I stared into the darkening street, concentrating on the blacker-than-shadow outlines of the trunks and branches of the maples. Did we reserve the decency that Canadians called tolerance for those to whom we were indifferent, releasing hatred on those whom we loved? Was hatred not only the reverse of love, but the deepest proof of its existence? Could we hate only those whom we loved, or wished to love? Or—I mustered the strength to stare in the face a conclusion I did not wish to reach—had Milly never loved me? Had it all been a charade undertaken to butter her ego with the ointments of cultural sophistication and sought-after diversity? It was possible, too, I conceded, that in promoting me, Milly had expected the southwestern Ontario lawyer's success to be local and limited. She might have been jealous that I had become a national figure. It was possible that she had craved an opportunity to put me in my place. Success was the prerogative of her all-star friends, in whose reflected light she basked. Her protégés could not outshine her.

I did not want to believe such slander. I remembered the promise of Milly's face in the candlelight. In all of my time in Canada—in all of my adult life—I had not been closer to anyone. With Chyou, I practised an eroticism of the body; Milly invested me with an eroticism of the spirit. And now she was gone. Could I win her back? I paced my flat until after midnight, sipping Cabernet not in celebration but in an embittered search for succour. I wondered how one contacted the president of the University of South Saskatchewan. If I could only speak to her.

It took me hours to fall asleep. I woke with a headache, ushered back into the daylight by the sweet scents of the bakery downstairs.

I rubbed my eyes and stared at the river. At the stroke of nine, I rang the Law Society of Upper Canada. I was passed from a secretary to a grave-sounding man who hummed and hawed. "Mr. Singh," he said. "The lay bencher on your panel happens to be in the office right now. I think he's best qualified to fill you in."

To my horror, a jovial Indian voice came on the line. Of course. This was Canada. No self-respecting institution would dare execute me unless a member of my own tribe were appointed to the firing squad. I knew that another Indian would be all too eager to worry out my faults. Certain he would be a jealous bastard, I longed for a triumvirate of circumspect Anglo-Saxons.

"I have to tell you, my friend," the fast-talking fellow said, after introducing himself as Dr. K. S. Sundaresan, a Toronto surgeon, "your case is looking very serious. Very serious indeed. We received two more complaints this morning."

"What? Who are these people? Why are they coming out of the woodwork?"

"I imagine it is because of the story in yesterday's *Toronto Star*."

"In the *Star*?"

"You didn't see the newspaper? Where have you been?"

"In Bombay," I said, hoping to strike a chord of fellow feeling. But, showing himself to be all business, the lay bencher wallah bored straight on. As I listened to him, I realized that the professor must have read the newspaper story. I had been so startled by his news that it hadn't occurred to me to ask him how he knew. If everyone in my village was equally well informed, my life would become unbearable.

"Two new complaints," Dr. K. S. Sundaresan

recited. He read out the names, pronouncing them correctly. "Both members of our community, Mr. Singh. Both claim that you cashed their cheques but did not perform the work contracted. Furthermore, that you failed to respond to repeated subsequent communications."

The names rang a remote bell. I feared that, as with Gita Kidambi, there might be sufficient truth to the dates and allegations to make me look bad. "Listen, my friend," I said, "I can clear this up. I have done nothing wrong. I've been very busy. In addition to my law practice, I have many public obligations—"

"I know that, Mr. Singh. You are the Canadian media's favourite Indian! Ha! Ha!"

I didn't like the sound of his laugh. "You cannot expect me to refuse such invitations," I said, trying to mollify the unforgiving fellow. "I realize it could as easily have been you as I, my friend, but you cannot expect me to rue good fortune. We came to this country to get ahead."

"Personally, I came to this country intending to respect its laws."

How humourless this Dr. K. S. Sundaresan was! What a prig! "My friend," I said, "you and I can reach an understanding." In India that is

precisely what we would have done. The understanding would have involved someone doing
him a favour; the possibilities would have been
implicit in his knowledge of who my father was,
in his being aware of the left-armed fast bowler's
stock-market prowess. But in Canada we could
not take such understanding for granted. In making the possibilities explicit, I would sound like a
low, untrustworthy fellow.

The net of Canadian legal life deprived us of
flexibility. I writhed against my new country. I
had barely opened my mouth when Dr. K. S. Sundaresan cut me off.

"If you continue to speak like that, there will
be fresh charges against you. I advise you to stick
to the matter at hand."

"Let me clear this up. I *can* clear it up. It is simply a question of my having been rather busy, and
of my having gone to India to visit my family. My
father is elderly. I'm sure you understand. I can sit
down and do this work in a matter of days."

"You could have done," he agreed.

"Then that is the solution, my friend. Simply
suspend me. Suspend me for two weeks. I will do
the work. At the end of the two weeks you rein-
state me, the work will be done, and my clients

will receive their services."

"As I say, Mr. Singh, we could have done this. Had you got in touch sooner. Now, however, it is too late."

"It is never too late when there is goodwill between men. Let me tell you, my friend, one thing I have learned in my public career is that with honest conversation and goodwill—"

"There is honest conversation and goodwill," Dr. K. S. Sundaresan said, "but there is also the law. The regulations governing the Law Society of Upper Canada dictate that once an investigation is undertaken, the object of the investigation may not resign his membership of the Law Society."

"I am not asking to resign. I am merely asking you to suspend me. This is not a resignation, it is a mere trifle—"

"According to the Law Society of Upper Canada, it is the same." How he loved the sound of his own voice rhyming out that title! I wanted to grit my teeth. "You are under investigation, Mr. Singh. At this stage there are only two possible outcomes: either you are exonerated or you are disbarred."

Staring at the river, I felt as though an evil bird were beating its wings in my chest. "How do I exonerate myself?" I said in a flat voice.

"You come to the hearing and defend yourself against the charges of professional misconduct that have been brought against you. That is the course open to you now, Mr. Singh."

I imagined myself facing a panel on which K. S. Sundaresan was the native informant. What an utter farce!

"I am not going to be judged by some god-damned kangaroo court. I am a man of substance. I have simply gotten behind on my work. You should ask yourself why this has happened, my friend. It has happened because I have been serving the community. I have been promoting better relations between the communities of our multi-cultural society. And you are going to punish me for that?"

"I know," the Toronto surgeon replied. "For that you were going to receive the Order of Canada."

"How do you know about that?" I could not control my voice. Heat prickled beneath my turban as though I were walking through the deserts of Rajasthan. The Order of Canada had been our secret. It was the consecration of my intimacy with Milly, our hidden-in-plain-sight public marriage ceremony. How could this pushy, jealous fellow besmirch the pinnacle of our concord? How could he even know about it?

"For a public man, Mr. Singh, you are not well informed. You should read the newspapers."

"That was in the newspapers? How do they know?"

"I only know what I read," the surgeon wallah said with a chuckle.

"I read the newspapers, too. How do you think I educated myself about this country's public life? But I have just returned from India. I am barely over my jetlag. Listen, my friend, my life has not always been easy. For my first ten years in Canada I did the most degrading work. I delivered pizzas, I placed notices on automobile windshields—"

"I am aware that you are a self-made man," Dr. K. S. Sundaresan said, "and not a natural leader of our community."

The bastard! It required little imagination to guess who he saw as our community's natural leader.

"In this country," I retorted, "the natural leader is the person who has climbed to the top in an atmosphere of freedom, not the person who was elevated by caste and class. You need to learn more about Canada, Dr. Sundaresan."

"I have also worked hard, Mr. Singh. I put my-self through medical school at the University of Toronto. Unlike you, I do not have a wealthy fa-ther."

He let this phrase hang in the air. Panic scrambled in my chest. Had this also been in the news-paper? I breathed hard, pacing my perch high over the rapids' tumult. My purchase felt uncer-tain, as though I might tumble straight through the window into the deep black water below me that turned translucent as it swooshed over the flat stones. Too distraught to reply, I let the si-lence go on and on.

"Assuming," Dr. Sundaresan said at last, "that you are the son of the man whose son I take you to be."

"You know who my father is?" My voice was a bleat.

"I think so. I am from New Delhi, but my un-cle does business in Bombay. I spent the summer prior to my departure for Canada as his assistant. I have met your brothers, Dr. Singh. If you are the Singh that I take you to be?"

"Why should there be any doubt?" I asked, my voice at once defiant and despairing.

"There might be doubt," he said, "because there are so many Singhs. And because in Canada you present yourself as a Sikh while in India your family are known to be Hindus."

No! I could not tolerate another threat to my dignity. I felt short of breath and overwhelmed by suffering. I longed—it may seem perverse—I longed for a wife to commiserate with me. I imagined myself levitating like a fakir over the rapids. In that second I grasped that I was a fissured being. I had divided myself. If it was true that Milly had betrayed me—a betrayal that seemed senseless and inconceivable, that I was certain would be cleared up the moment I spoke to her—then I was a man pared from his own soul. I was a body without purpose or impulse. Even my public life—particularly my public life—lacked rhyme or reason unless Milly was there to witness and approve of it.

I did not want to discuss the religious guise I had chosen for my public being. That was no one's business but my own. "That is a complicated story, Dr. Sundaresan."

"I am sure it is, Mr. Singh," he said in an unctuous voice.

"Here we are discussing a different question.

Here we are discussing my suspension from the Law Society of Upper Canada so that I can clear up some work on which I have lamentably fallen behind schedule. Once I have done the work in which I have been remiss, we may all go on with our lives."

"You know that suspension is impossible, Mr. Singh. You have only one option and that is to come to the hearing in Toronto and defend yourself."

"And if I don't come? Then you cannot proceed with your hearing."

"If you don't come, we proceed with the hearing in your absence—but in the presence, I assure you, of the city's media. If you are not here to defend yourself, it is certain that you will be disbarred."

TWELVE
can you forgive her?

I put down the receiver. With Dr. K. S. Sundaresan serving as lay bencher, I did not doubt the outcome of the disciplinary panel. I longed to phone Esther. Having come closer than any other woman to being my wife, she would offer me the counsel I needed—provided her job, her husband, and her children allowed her to do so. I suspected she would tell me that I must fight this. I must struggle. I must launch a campaign denouncing the charges against me as racism, as a vast right-wing conspiracy against the crusading southwestern Ontario lawyer, and enlist my literary allies to sign open letters. I must up the ante and go on television to denounce my persecutors. The mere thought exhausted me.

The indignity of struggle would disturb my quest for tranquillity. These were the tactics of a rabble-rouser. I aspired to a serene dignity, to the calm of the drawing room, where a gentleman could confer in peace with other men of his rank. To fray my Victorian remove from the vulgar toil of the street in order to save my position was no salvation at all. I would save myself by continuing to be the person I wished to be.

Only once in my life had I exerted myself, and that was at law school. I had been younger then, I had been willing to take desperate remedies to escape the towers beyond the end of the subway line, and, after the first few weeks, Esther had been at my side. As I picked my way down the outdoor staircase, I recognized, against my will, that it was my insistence on being the person whom I wished to be and no one else that had landed me in this fix. A man who gloried less in the pomp and circumstance of being R. U. Singh would have made the effort to go through his mail upon his return from speaking engagements and panel discussions. He would have put in the arduous late-night hours of work that were necessary to complete the perfunctory legal chores for which he had been contracted by the likes of

Gita Kidambi. Rather than idealizing his connection to Milly as a dream that could go on forever, and refusing to sully it with a sordid separation agreement, he would have been realistic enough to grasp that the only thing that mattered when one had a friend as powerful as Millicent Crowe was to continue, at all costs, to be her friend, and to do her all the favours she requested. I had been blind and foolish. Yet, as with my turban, this was *my* blindness, *my* foolishness. Exhaustion drained me. I clung to the metal railing like an old man.

I opened the door of the bakery café. It was before ten o'clock. The day's crop of tourists had not yet arrived from Toronto; only locals sat at the tables. I was glad to see that the professor was not among them. As I stepped in the door, the café went silent. The girl behind the counter— she was married now, with a ring on her finger— pressed her lips together in a smile that grew long and stiff. I bowed my head and shuffled among the newspapers on the tables, looking in vain for the previous day's *Toronto Star*.

I approached the counter. The girl leaned forward, whispering. "Don't worry, Mr. Singh. As soon as I saw that article, I pulled that section of the paper off the tables."

"Do you still have it? You see, I haven't read it."
She looked pained. "I'll see if I can find it."

She returned looking abashed, waved me to a vacant table in the protective shadow of the counter, and brought me a coffee without my having ordered one. As soon as I read the article, I understood why those parts of my life that I had assumed to be private were now public.

> Accusations of malpractice and misappropriation of funds swirled around the southwestern Ontario lawyer R. U. Singh yesterday as he faced allegations of professional misconduct from two of his clients, one of them a prominent university administrator. Ms. Gita Kidambi of Kitchener, Ont., and Dr. Millicent Crowe, recently named President of the University of South Saskatchewan ... According to reliable sources, Mr. Singh, a noted champion of race relations, was due to receive the Order of Canada. It is understood that his name has been withdrawn from consideration.

I whimpered. I could not help myself. I kept my head down, concentrating on the page, aware that the other clients were observing every twitch of my hunched body. My secret marriage to Milly had been demolished in the most demeaning public way. Seeing my name linked in print with the Order of Canada confirmed our special, surreptitious relationship even as I was deprived of both the honour and Milly.

I got to my feet and, keeping my head lowered, left the café without finishing my coffee. I did not thank the young woman who had been so attentive to me. My mind was in an uproar. Who had done this? I could not believe that Milly had given this information to the *Toronto Star*. Had my procrastination over her separation agreement, my departure on my trip, caused her such grief? I had my doubts about the professor's story that Milly had called the campus police to remove her husband; but if she had, her position would have been weakened by the absence of a separation agreement. The inconvenience would have irritated her, no doubt, but would the irritation have been great enough for her to betray our friendship? I could not believe that my village neighbour, the foundation of my cultured country life, was no longer mine, or that she had announced our breakup by publically striking my name from the list vof those under consideration for the Order of Canada. This sordid public debasement smacked of the machinations of Milly's enemies. I suspected the scruffy professor himself of planting the information.

I climbed the stairs to my flat. My first thought was to call Milly's real-estate agent. I knew the fellow, as one professional in a village is acquainted with another. He answered his phone on the first ring. Before I had time to think how best to phrase my query, I was stammering my name.

"R. U.!" the affable fellow said. "What can I do for you?"

"I am aware that you sold Millicent Crowe's house. I'm waiting for some documents and a letter from her, but in the meantime I don't have a current phone number. I was wondering—"

"All I've got is her office number. I figured if anybody had the home number, it would be you."

"A temporary inconvenience," I murmured, "due to the suddenness of her move. She's sending me her new phone numbers with the documents." My voice piped up, as thin and brave as that of a schoolboy who, in spite of knowing that the master is skeptical of his story and may even cane him, decides to stick to it. Beneath my tremor, I heard the gulf of my longing and my need for Milly.

"Sure, R. U., I understand." I feared that he understood too much. He gave me the phone number of the president's office at the University of South Saskatchewan. I thanked him, hoping I did not sound excessively grateful. I walked around the flat and looked out the inland window that gave over the hill away from the river. The two-storey houses of red brick and washed-out limestone stared at me through their blank, squared-off windows, dim with knowledge of my humiliations. My breath trembled in my chest. I dialled the Saskatchewan area code, then the number.

"President's Office," said a voice, broader and more Western than those to which I had grown accustomed.

"I'd like to speak to Milly Crowe, please."

"President Crowe is in a meeting. Would you like to leave a message?"

"Yes," I said, my voice growing more resolute. "Please ask President Crowe to ring R. U. Singh, Attorney at Law."

"Atturnawah? How do you spell that? Is that

an Indian name?"

"Yes."

"If you're a member of the Cree band calling about the land claim, I have to tell you that the university is directing all communications from our legal team to yours. Please stop harassing President Crowe. Have a good day——"

"I am not that sort of Indian," I said in haste. "I am a friend of Milly's from Ontario."

"You don't sound like you're from Ontario." A suspicious pause. "How do you spell that name again?"

"Singh. S-i-n-g-h."

"What sort of name is that?"

"Indian," I said. "From India." I felt myself slipping down an abyss. Racist poison, my daily bitter cordial during my years in Toronto, when on bad days it had seemed that my name was *Paki,* surged back. Not that this plague had gone away: I myself had simply ceased to be an object of disdain by ascending into a milieu where prejudice was displaced by the genteel desire to socialize with diversity. This woman's belligerence was a foretaste of the disrespect that awaited me if I lost my privileges. The thought twisted the tourniquet of my unease one notch tighter.

I explained to the receptionist that "Attorney-at-Law" was my profession, not my name. I told her that Milly knew my phone number by heart, then gave it to her anyway. She informed me that if President Crowe wished to speak to me, I would receive a phone call from the president's executive assistant to schedule my conversation with the president.

It did not sound promising.

I put down the receiver, longing for fresh air. I started towards the door, then stopped. Much as a walk along the river would do me good, I felt apprehensive about stepping outside. I tried to remember how many of my fellow villagers had seen me in the bakery café. Five? Six? If each of them related the incident to three or four people, and each of those people spoke to three or four others, the whole village would know of my disaster within hours. I would no longer stroll these streets as country squire but as cunning pariah. Why, *why* had Milly done this? I could not accept that she had renounced our tender, teasing friendship. Surely her decision to complain about my indolence to the Law Society of Upper Canada was a mere fit of pique whose consequences she had not foreseen. She did not, I told myself, know the legal world; she could not have calculated—

Yet if there was one ability in which Millicent Crowe excelled, it was calculation. She must have known that this accusation would destroy me. It must have been she, who had nominated me for the Order of Canada, who had also withdrawn my nomination. Who else but she could have alerted the newspaper? The selection process for the Order was confidential. No one but Milly could have provided this information to the *Star*.

Had our friendship meant nothing? How could moments as vital with companionship as our evening in Montreal leave no enduring residue? It made me question whether every experience of intimacy was not ultimately meaningless. I still chuckled at the memory of a man suggesting that my beard was false, that I was a woman in drag. In spite of being wrong, in his remark's deeper implications, the man had been right. I was in drag: as a Sikh, as a Canadian, as a person of singular achievements. Milly and I shared the charade of playing the part of eminent people at festivals and conferences, yet neither of us had written eminent literary works like the guests at Milly's long oak table. The man had been right, too, about the dynamics of our couple: practical

Milly, in her slacks and pantsuits, incarnated the male principle; I, with my mooning over books, my scarves and flowing jackets, my conditioned lack of self-assertion, was the wife.

Milly had known this. She had known that if she hit me, I would not hit back. My worshipful adoration prevented it, as did my passive nature. All day I paced my flat, sipped wine, quailed at the thought of walking the streets beneath my neighbours' eyes, and hoped against hope that I would receive a phone call informing me that President Crowe of the University of South Saskatchewan wished to schedule a conversation with me. The first time the phone rang, I jumped. It was a *Toronto Star* reporter. I refused to do an interview. I began vetting my calls. Most were mere annoyances from call centres in Lahore; there was no call from Milly.

I slept badly. In the morning, my mood worsened. I had barely dressed when I heard a knock on the door. When I opened it, the girl from the bakery café handed me a newspaper. Her eyes lowered, she said: "I'm giving this to you, Mr. Singh, instead of leaving it on the table." She hesitated. "I'm sorry." Without meeting my eyes, she turned away. Her steps, descending the stairs, punctuated the gush of the rapids.

I shut the door and returned to the kitchen. I drank a coffee and listened to the morning news. As long as I did not open the newspaper, the calamities it contained would not wound me; the life I had built remained intact.

Accepting for the first time that my comfortable life was imperilled, I yearned to savour it for a few minutes longer. At last I opened the newspaper. I reconciled myself to confronting more evidence that Milly was no longer on my side, even though I still could not believe that the woman I worshipped, who had given me my start, had undermined me.

The newspaper took me by surprise. A headline halfway down page seven of the front section read: EMBATTLED LAWYER ACCUSED OF CULTURAL APPROPRIATION.

Representatives of Toronto's Hindu and Sikh communities joined forces yesterday to issue a declaration denouncing the southwestern Ontario lawyer R. U. Singh, a well-known figure in debates about multiculturalism. Mr. Singh is currently facing disciplinary action from the Law Society of Upper Canada on charges of professional misconduct and misappropriation of funds stemming from accusations that he failed to deliver legal services for which he had been contracted.

Now fresh accusations against Mr. Singh have surfaced.

The community organizations allege that Mr. Singh, who makes his public appearances wearing a Sikh turban, is, in fact, a Hindu.

"We know his family in India and they are all Hindus," said T. N. Singh, speaking on behalf of Sikhs of Toronto. "It's an insult to our faith for him to dress as one of us when he belongs to a different religion. What does he think this is—Halloween?"

Hindus, too, are furious with Mr. Singh, who they see as having abandoned his culture. "He is a traitor," said Raj Patel, the Canadian representative for the Hindu nationalist party, BJP. "When we come to Canada, we leave our country but we do not leave our culture. It is the duty of every person to honour his true identity. Mr. Singh's stunts have insulted Hindus all around the world. He owes it to his community, and to the family that raised him, to be authentic. When he comes to Toronto to be disciplined, we will be there to show him what we think of him."

Professor Vikram Gupta, a specialist in South Asian politics at York University, explained that in India …

K. S. Sundaresan, I thought, *you are a fucking bastard*! If only I could prove that he had compromised his partiality as a lay bencher! If I could pin this leak on him, I would sink his pathetic, upwardly mobile little career. I phoned the Law Society and shouted out my accusations. For once I was not passive. I took the initiative, as I had on the day that I first stepped into Milly's garden.

"That man exceeded his authority," I said, "and now he has divulged details of my private life to the newspapers! Your disciplinary hearing is null and void! Let me finish my work and then we will have our hearing. But we will have it without that treacherous son of a bitch K. S. Sundaresan! I demand that a different lay bencher be appointed."

"Dr. Sundaresan," a tombstone voice replied, "was appointed out of cultural sensitivity—"

"Fuck cultural sensitivity," I said. "Can't we just have culture?"

"That statement," the man from the Law Society said, "is unworthy of a gentleman in your position."

Was he referring to my status as an immigrant and a person of colour? This was an elite form of racism, no better than the University of South Saskatchewan telephone receptionist's disdain. I hesitated. Yet perhaps he was right; perhaps I shouldn't have said what I had. After all, I did want people to be culturally sensitive. I had built my life by fulfilling this yearning. I remonstrated that I would not be able to attend my hearing because my personal security had been threatened by the Hindu fundamentalists of the BJP. Look at the morning paper, I said; it's there in black and white. They're going to try to get me.

"I read that article," the implacable legal voice responded. "In a democracy, everyone has the right to peaceful protest. No one has threatened your physical security, Mr. Singh. I look forward to seeing you at the hearing."

I had scarcely hung up the phone when the damned thing rang again. I did not answer it: not that day nor on any of the days that followed. I let the messages pile up until my inbox was full. I did not listen to the messages, or call anyone back. There was only one person I wanted to hear from, and I knew that she was not going to return my call.

THIRTEEN
the woman in white

On the day of my hearing, I refused to get out of bed. If I got out of bed, I might get dressed. If I got dressed, I might get in my car and drive to Toronto. I was curious about the hearing and longed to denounce the lies that would be told against me. I wondered whether Milly would appear to present her testimony. No, I knew her well enough to be certain that she would not expose herself. If I went, I would not meet Milly; I would be surrounded by BJP fanatics denouncing me for having abandoned authentic Hinduism. I would have to watch Dr. K. S. Sundaresan smirk— I had never seen the man's face, yet his voice told me that he would smirk—as he took infinite pleasure in snuffing out my career. A bottomless blackness opened at my feet. This morning my career, my life, my public self—"the southwestern Ontario lawyer," that externalized identity which, reversing its flow, had seeped into my intimate being to become the fibre of my existence—would be exterminated. I rolled over on my stomach and buried my head beneath the sheets. I lay inert for seconds, minutes, hours, impervious to the sunlight that angled over the lip of the ravine. I drifted in and out of consciousness. My unconscious moments felt more like a mystic's trance, or the dazed incomprehension of a survivor of war, than ordinary sleep.

When the phone rang, it was already ten-thirty. I scrambled out of bed.

"R. U.?" It was the CBC reporter I had met in the atrium. I was glad it was someone I knew, rather than an anonymous, predatory voice. A contradictory wave of relief rushed through me, evoking a sentimental companionship with this man who was one of the many friends and acquaintances I had made in a world which had become mine without my having expected it, and which I was now in danger of losing.

"What happened?" I asked.

"You're finished. I'm sorry, man. There was

nobody there to defend you. The evidence was all on one side."

"What evidence?" I asked.

"Three of them testified. All long distance by speakerphone."

"Was Milly one of them?"

"Millicent Crowe from South Saskatchewan? Yeah. Can you tell me about that? I thought she was part of that gang you hang out with. What happened?"

"I have no idea." I bit my lip, realizing I was more upset than I could possibly understand. I fought to control myself. "I suggest you ask her."

"Hey, maybe I will. I have to tell you, R. U., it was quite a scene. There were Indian guys outside with placards saying you hated your culture or ranting about cultural appropriation—all kinds of crazy stuff. Can you clear that up for me: are you a Hindu or a Sikh?"

"I was a Hindu in India. In Canada I am a Sikh. I do not apologize for that. It is in the nature of immigration that the immigrant reinvents himself."

"Okay. Thanks." I imagined him copying down the quote. "After the testimony, they went out then they turned around and came back in. It took eleven minutes. That's all. Eleven minutes and they disbarred you."

I winced at his utterance of the fatal word.

"Could I have your reaction, R. U.?"

"How can I react? I don't know how to react. I don't know how to deal with this. It's as though they've taken away my soul."

"Thanks." He was taking notes again.

I was sick of this man. I wanted to get him off the line. I knew the others would be worse, but he was making me ill. I ended the conversation and hung up the phone. I sat down. I was no longer a lawyer. What could I do? In an access of desperation, I phoned Davies and asked for Esther. I left a message with her administrative assistant, asking her to call me back. I waited for her call.

Sitting on my bed in my pyjamas, I felt ravaged by isolation. I pressed the button on my answering machine. *You have twenty-three new messages.*

First message: "Hi, Mr. Singh, this is Jamie from *What's New This Morning*. Just to let you know that we've had a programming change and won't be needing you for the panel on the seventeenth. Thanks a lot. Have a great day."

The messages continued.

"Hello, Mr. Singh, this is Rubicon Collegiate. We've decided that a different speaker will fit better with the themes of our multicultural festival. Our students are proud of their identities."

"You are a self-hating Hindu. You think you are a Sikh? We will stick a *kirpan* in your fucking traitor body!"

"Hi, R. U., this is Ahmed from Multicultural Television. Listen, I've just come from a meeting and we've decided it's best for all concerned if we suspend your column for a month. I'm sure you understand. We're taking a wait-and-see approach here. We can talk later, okay?"

"You think you are a Sikh? You think a Sikh is just dressing up? You remember Air India? That is what will happen to you, my friend."

"Mr. Singh, this is Captain John Wilson from the Police Services Board. I'm afraid I have to ask you not to attend the next meeting of the committee on police-community relations. Pending the outcome of your hearing—"

The outcome of my hearing was now public information. In eleven minutes I had ceased to be the southwestern Ontario lawyer R. U. Singh. The personage whose life I had enacted without ever fully inhabiting him had vanished. As I listened to cautious Canadians scurrying for cover and obstreperous Indians howling threats, I prepared myself for the next wave. For a few deluded moments after my conversation with the reporter, I had imagined that I could transition from my legal life to a career as a full-time commentator, television personality, and journalist. As I listened to my messages, this last hope crumbled.

The tape ran out in the middle of howled curses in Hindi. I erased it. I did so just in time. The phone began to ring again. In no mood to answer, I listened to the messages as they came in. The calls were from reporters requesting interviews. A few latecomers rang with contrite cancellations of invitations to speak or appear on panels. I stayed in my apartment, not daring to show my face in the village where I had once strolled down the street with the proud gait of a squire. No one phoned to commiserate, express sympathy, or see how I was feeling. The phone rang and rang, devastating messages piling up one after another until the answering machine tape was full again. I erased it. By late afternoon, the gap between calls had grown longer. By evening, I was almost forgotten.

In the morning, the final wave of opprobrium struck: FedExes, courier messages, and registered letters that required signatures on receipt obliged me to open the door. Legal documents, ejecting me from the charitable boards on which I sat, were thrust into my hands. One after another, my retainers were cancelled. With each envelope brought to my door by a shambling figure in uniform, I watched ten thousand or twenty thousand dollars in annual income vanish. Two days after my hearing, I was destitute. I could no longer practise law, I was no longer welcome as a journalist or commentator, and my retainers had been cut off. I had money in the bank, but no way of making more. Without having read them, I knew that the major newspapers had trumpeted my disgrace. My refusal to do interviews would not have changed that. Some helpful soul slid a copy of the village weekly into my mailbox. This quaint six-page publication, which normally mingled accounts of the town council's discussions of property taxes with photographs of local lads who had been invited to try out for NHL teams, had got on the story quickly. My face was at the top of the front page. LOCAL LAWYER DISGRACED.

I had to leave. To flee my village, as Fielding's Tom Jones had done. That evening, I phoned my Shanghai widow. Like my cousin in his tower, Chyou did not read Canadian newspapers or watch Canadian television. Having no idea what had happened to me, she received me with her customary charm. Talking to her was like entering the Good Kingdom. I felt a surge of hope. It was still possible for me to dwell in an unblemished past. If Chyou received me with such candour, others might, too. I asked her if I could spend a day and a night with her, maybe two. She laughed like the sheltered young girl she had been decades ago. "So you are eager to see me."

"Yes, I am." For the first time in days my voice felt steady.

She told me I would be welcome. Knowing that there would be no return after this departure, I packed my belongings. I would come back to the village to clear out my flat, but I could not live here again. From now on, my credentials were: *Squire (failed)*, *Southwestern Ontario Lawyer (failed)*. Only as a fugitive, that identity I had refined in tandem with Milly, did I remain active. After all that had happened, I would be a fugitive forever in the circles where I had been famous: a fugitive who had been expelled from being a fugitive. I had belonged to Milly's rural aristocracy as long as I had snapped to attention like a brown-skinned bellhop to carry out the chores that were necessary to advance her friends' careers. In retrospect, I saw that they had underestimated the consequences of my lawsuit against the prime minister; it had given me recognition, money, power, and an autonomy that dethroned their certainties. One of their protégés had slipped the leash, growing nearly as powerful as they.

As I rose in the darkness of a Saturday morning, a dozen tiny incidents pestered my brain: novels I had read that Milly, the English professor, had not; my idenfication of a quote uttered by a British writer who had joined us at the long oak table one summer, which drew blank looks from famous Canadian writers; a time when she had said to me, "Of course everybody knows who you are. You're always on television!" Milly's resentments flared in the night of my memory like an uneven row of torches. I had been so intoxicated by the miracle of our companionship that I had failed to appreciate that miracles are precarious. I had recognized the volatility of my flirtation with my woman in white, how it teetered on an emotional tightrope where it could neither remain simply a friendship nor plunge into a full-blown affair. Naive colonial that I was, I had failed to see that relationships that are volatile rarely last long. I had not realized how much she resented my success.

I zipped my bags. Knowing that I would soon be with my sensuous Chyou, with whom from the beginning my entente had been of body with body, I performed my ablutions, as my favourite novels referred to them, with precision. It was still dark outside when I carried one large bag then the other down the outdoor staircase to my parking space near the river. The outdoor air drilled cold into me. After days stuck in my stuffy apartment, where I had eaten little but rice, the morning chill seemed, paradoxically, to enlarge each pore of my flesh. It rendered me as alert in my body as I would have liked to be in my spirit.

I climbed the stairs again for two smaller bags. The scent of bread in the oven wafted from the bakery. I locked the door and hurried back down the stairs to my car before anyone could spot me. Above the bluff on the opposite side of the ravine, a wash of paler sky scythed into the blackness. I listened to the rapids for a second, then slipped into my car and drove down the street, and across the bridge where streetlights shined down on the weir.

I drove into the countryside.

Barely an hour and a half later, I parked in

front of Chyou's squat red-brick house, its roof pitched as low as that of a Buddhist temple. It was not yet breakfast time.

Chyou lived two blocks north of the Danforth. Years ago, with the help of a legacy from her husband and a bank loan, she had opened a manicure and pedicure business between a souvlaki house and a Lebanese pita takeaway on the Greek neighbourhood's main thoroughfare. Hiring girls from the Philippines to do the work, she had managed her investment with an astute eye. Five years later, she had opened a second shop on the edge of Chinatown. Though our intimacy did not extend to financial revelations, it was clear that she was prospering.

She met me at the door in the sporty style she adopted on weekends: white running shoes, black spandex leggings, and a thigh-length white dress. My other woman in white, the one who had not betrayed me. Seeing that I was not myself, she made me a breakfast of toast, kalamata paste, and Chinese dumplings, then led me to a back room where she sat me in an armchair, and removed my shoes and socks. She dunked my feet in a small bucket of warm water, rubbed oils into my skin, then flayed my soles with a pumice stone. It was a delicious sensation: a blend of caning and kissing that relieved me of a husk of my being.

As Chyou worked on my feet, I stared across the room at the decorations on her living room wall: Chinese prints of men and women's bodies entwined, a photograph of arid ruins overlooking a pellucid Aegean bay that reminded me of my history lessons at the Academy. I murmured formless expressions of gratitude. Chyou smiled. We moved to her bedroom and rubbed oils into each other's bodies. In contrast to Esther, whose body had slid out of my view when we made love, Chyou's lusty eagerness, which belied the delicacy of her proportions, made her utterly present. I inhabited her as I inhabited the world. She was a southern woman, darker skinned than most of the Chinese people I saw in Toronto. But for a coppery underlay in her complexion, our skin tones would have been very similar. Her sports gear emphasized a tapered litheness that refuted the initial impression of a petite East-Asian woman. Waking close to noon to find that we were still in bed together, I felt a gush of relief. No one who knew of my disgrace could find me in this place. I reached for Chyou again.

"You are a greedy man," she said.

"Infinitely greedy."

She slid into my arms.

It was a lovely day. Late that afternoon I spoiled it by asking her to marry me.

"R. U., what's wrong with you?" Her tone was forgiving, yet I saw that I had upset our accord. Her shoulders had stiffened. "You know that is not how it is between us."

We were sitting at her kitchen table sipping Chinese tea. The moment was so idyllic that I wished to hold it forever. Was that why I had made my impulsive declaration? As I saw Chyou get to her feet and pace with an impatience that I had not provoked in her before, I realized that I had been trying to turn the diaphanousness of longing into a palpable object; to freeze in place an eroticism that thrived on changeability. I needed both Milly of the fugitive spirit with the immigrant's drive for institutional acceptance, and Chyou of the generous body and diffident independence, who had made it on her own terms. Each had nurtured me; both had refused to become mine alone. I needed these two women to weigh on opposite flanks of my being to sustain my equilibrium of body and mind.

Having lost Milly, I was off balance. My mind

was making serious missteps.

I regretted my words, but it was too late. Chyou was troubled, even offended. "I said you could stay for two nights, R. U., but do not try to stay longer. I will not let you bind my feet. I specialize in setting the feet free."

"I'm sorry."

"How could you say something like that?" She leaned her hips against the kitchen counter. I sensed her desire to back even farther away from me. "I thought we understood each other."

"We do understand each other, Chyou. I'm sorry. Please take my declaration as a compliment and not a threat."

"I take it as a sign that you don't understand me the way I thought you did. I will tell you something, R. U. The year after my husband's death was the worst time of my life. But the years since I've gotten used to being a widow have been my best days. I would never have left my husband, but now I would never go back to being married. Marriage is not good for women; it stops them from doing too many things."

"I know, Chyou. Forget what I said. Please take it as a moment's madness, an excessive declaration of how much I appreciate you."

"I can try. I thought you and I understood each other. Now I have doubts."

I offered her a night on the town, of the sort I had courted her with when we first met: dinner in Yorkville, a show on King Street West, late-night drinks at the top of the Park Plaza Hotel. She demurred. We stayed home and watched a video. She went to bed before me. I sat in the living room, reading William Wilkie Collins. On Sunday morning, as she was making toast and eggs to eat with the rest of the kalamata paste, she said: "You know what my name means, don't you, R. U.? 'Chyou' is 'sweet autumn.' I am not yet at autumn in my life, but when I get there I want it to be sweet, not ruined by a stale marriage."

"Chyou, please, I understand."

"I still cannot believe that you asked me that. I thought you knew me!"

On Sunday the Danforth manicure and pedicure shop opened at noon. Chyou was in the habit of going in on Sunday morning to do inventory. "Girls from the Philippines are just Spanish enough to steal from me if I don't keep track of the materials and the money." She smiled and kissed me. After she left, I sat reading in her living room. I realized how unaccustomed I was to being in this house; I had scarcely ever spent time here during the day. Chyou and I did not know each other in our workaday lives. If I had nourished foolish illusions about her, she, too, had been deluded to imagine that I was a man who understood her.

Too agitated to read, I put my book down. I played with the remote control of the television set. When I pressed the button, the television lit up on a station where a newsreader was speaking what I took to be Cantonese. I flipped around, looking for the CBC. The news was on. I watched the prime minister—a new prime minister (though he was old) who had succeeded the man against whom I had brought my case—speaking in English with a heavy French-Canadian accent. Political stories gave way to human-interest pieces that took place farther from the nation's capital.

Then, to my horror, my photograph appeared on the screen.

I felt so sick that I barely heard the announcer's words as she reeled out a biased account of my humiliations. I saw her smirk beneath her blond hair—was it a wig?—as she reported that the southwestern Ontario lawyer, noted promoter of multiculturalism, had been disbarred. And now, it emerged, he had always been a fake, a confidence trickster who had conned the nation in its honest search for authentic identities. Though he wore a turban, lawyer Singh was not a Sikh. The blonde cut away to a rugged-looking male reporter standing in front of a chipped rock face.

"I'm here in Thunder Bay, Ontario," the male reporter said, holding a microphone in front of his mouth, "where a local woman says that R. U. Singh adopted Sikh dress because he wanted to marry her. Mrs. Seema Robinson, now married with three children, says that when she was a teenager, R. U. Singh came to her house to court her."

An Indian woman approaching forty, wearing a white T-shirt, appeared on the screen. She sat in a small kitchen; lanky light-brown teenagers lounged around her in attitudes of impatience. "My father ran an Indian takeaway. R. U. was a foreign student. He was lonely and my father took him under his wing. I was sixteen. R. U. was very traditional, he was looking for a traditional Indian wife and he began courting me. Life in Canada confused him, but he was always respectful.

I can't believe they've kicked him out of being a lawyer."

Her puzzled face gave way to that of the reporter. "According to Mrs. Robinson, it was her father, a practising Sikh who died with her mother in the Air India tragedy, who taught R. U. Singh to tie a turban. He hoped the young man would convert to Sikhism and marry his daughter."

A photograph of S. A. and his wife flashed across the screen, then vanished.

"He was supposed to convert," Seema said in a halting voice. "But he never did. We never got engaged. He got scared and ran away to Toronto. I can't believe he went around all those years pretending to be a Sikh." Her eyes glinted; her children looked embarrassed.

"And so," the reporter concluded, the wind blowing off Lake Superior ruffling his hair, "one woman's youthful broken heart sheds light on a once-famous media commentator's disgrace—"

I clicked off the television. Liars! What unconscionable falsehoods they peddled. And they said that I was not true to myself? I was so upset that a vein began to throb in my temple. I went to the kitchen, ran a glass of water and sat down in the leather chair where Chyou had massaged my feet.

Once I had calmed down, I devoted a few minutes to dwelling on the memory of my friend S. A. and lamenting his terrible demise. I could only suppose that the shock of her parents' death had unhinged Seema.

Chyou came back at three in the afternoon. Her head was lowered. A free newspaper that Toronto commuters read on the subway drooped from her hand. She stalked towards me. As she looked up, I saw that her eyes were glassy.

"You did not tell me that you had lost your profession. You wanted to marry me because you are poor now!"

She held up the paper, showing me a headline: DISGRACED LAWYER PRETENDED TO BE SIKH.

"You pretended to be someone else." She stamped her foot. "You didn't take your culture seriously. That is not for me! I thought you and I were proud of our cultures—"

"You are Canadian, Chyou. You've been here for more than half your life."

She waved the newspaper at me. "I am pure Chinese. But you!"

"You speak English—and Cantonese, not Mandarin—you eat Greek food, you work with girls from the Philippines. You have an Indian man in your bed! You've reinvented yourself. As you had to. People who don't reinvent themselves don't survive." My mind trawled from the late Sam Singh of Thunder Bay to my cousin in his tower to Milly's husband. I remembered the writer from the Deep South, the last time I had spoken to him in his house, wondering about Milly's next move. "I've done the same. We can be proud of ourselves."

"I am proud of being Chinese. Nobody who is not Chinese understands my identity."

Then why are you with me? I wanted to ask. But my position was already precarious. "The kids don't care," I said. It was a phrase I had used on television panels. "Look at the children on the street. Even when their parents are from the same culture, they are a mixture of one thing and another. They don't care where people come from."

Her tiny mouth flexed. She stepped forward and took my hand. "R. U., how could you pretend to be of one religion when you belonged to another?" Her hand reached up and gave my turban a derogatory tug. "How could you hide from me that you had lost your profession when you asked to marry me?"

"After the last week, you're all I have left. Chyou, I wanted to hold onto you."

"So that I could support you like a child? Neither of us has children, R. U. That's why I do not care what the kids think. I will never be a Canadian kid or have a Canadian kid. I will always be an immigrant. I like hard work and honour and loyalty to my culture. I thought you did, too."

Her words brought us to an impasse. We stood in her kitchen holding hands. I had too many problems that were mine alone to solve problems that Chyou and I shared. I bowed my head and released her fingers.

FOURTEEN
new grub street

To be a man without a profession is to know that you must make your own way. I told myself that I would have a handsome send-off. When I emptied my savings account in the village, the clerk I had known for years serving me with averted eyes, I left with a bank draft that was nearly six figures. Even so, I realized that I had not managed my funds well. If I had bought a house when the prime minister had spoken my name, then resold it now, I would have been comfortable for years to come. I had assumed my media popularity would last forever; I had taken for granted that I would always be a lawyer. Now I had sufficient funds to keep me going, in the most modest of lives, for no more than three years. I had a name that had been dragged through the mud, and the eternal loathing of countless Indians. I was a pariah among my own people, and an unperson among the chattering classes. My formal credentials had been obliterated. I was *B.A., M.A. (failed) Bombay (ranked equivalent to Ontario Grade Twelve), B.A. Lakehead (dropped out), LL.B. Western (nullified by disbarment), Q.C. (rescinded), O.C. (cancelled).* I was no longer an educated professional. All that remained was my experience as a migrant.

I migrated again.

In Canada, as in India, the quickest migration is internal. Uneasy following the youthful tides west, I inverted the movement of history and drove east. I left Chyou's house in the evening and returned to the village. I sorted essential possessions from mere trifles of which the Buddhists would counsel me to let go. The village was silent except for the sound of the rapids. I saw no one I knew.

When my car was packed, I drank a strong Darjeeling tea and wrote a letter to my landlord to tell him I was leaving. I asked him to sell my table, chairs, bed, couch and television. I wrote him a cheque for the last month's rent; I wrote cheques for the utility bills. Only after all my envelopes were ready did it occur to me that I could not buy postage stamps in the middle of the night. I laid the envelopes on the front seat of my car.

I had thought I would drive all night, but by the time I reached Kingston, I was swerving out of my lane. I turned onto the off-ramp, booked into a motel, and slept. In my light, fitful sleep, I struggled with the thought that in the Victorian novels I read, people were shackled by their identities. They kept their accents and class identities, even as their fates rose and fell. In contrast to the plays of Shakespeare, identities were fixed: people were rarely in disguise or in drag, no man was mistaken for a woman; society was vast and all-encompassing, and the only way to be reborn was to emigrate to Australia. I wanted to anchor myself in a world with that same degree of stability, yet I needed to fix my stability in a place where no one would recognize my most stable, once-famous self. Like Chyou, who rode at the front of my mind in a patchwork of mingled memories of fleshly passion and bitter parting, I wanted things that contradicted each other. I woke at noon to a grey sky and drove down into the centre of the dark limestone city of Kingston in search of a post office. I watched students wandering the streets in their Queen's University jackets. I mailed my envelopes, then kept walking until I reached a bridge that crossed a strait that fed into Lake Ontario. In the middle of the bridge, I unwound my turban, tugged off my turban cap, and threw them both into the water, imagining the Hindus and Sikhs of Toronto cheering in triumph as I did so.

The turban unravelled as it floated towards the lake. Yet my foes should not imagine that I had given up on self-reinvention. I shook out my hair, then walked back into the city centre that was a magnified version of my limestone village. I looked for a hairdresser. Nearly twenty-five years earlier I had gone out to look for a barber and had taken a wrong turn. Now I would complete that curtailed walk in the snow.

"Take it all off," I said to the middle-aged barber, who had hesitated when I sat down. "Give me the haircut you give to the boys from the military academy." Fifteen minutes later, I peered into the mirror he held up to my face. The grey military crewcut that crouched on the crown of my head made the beard spilling over my jowls look dishevelled. "Now shave me."

"Holy cow. Not even your wife's gonna recognize you."

"Sometimes that is a good thing!" We laughed like men who meet at a bar. The breath of male companionship hauled me back from the abyss of exile. I enjoyed the feeling of lather on my cheeks, the lethal perfection of the straight razor: I had not seen one in years. When I looked in the mirror for the second time, I saw that the fellow staring back at me had endured hard times: his eyes were baggy, his dewlaps drooped, the skin that had been covered by a beard was of a sallow, unburnished brown.

"You look great," the barber said. After he untied my bib, I stood up like a toddler taking his first steps. I paid him and gave him a generous tip. "Thanks, man," he said. "What's your name?"

"Richard. My friends call me Ric." We shook hands. I refused to concede victory to my enemies. In my ability to start again, I was rich in potential, a winner. And with my large, frank face and burly brush cut, I looked like a Ric. I resembled a garage mechanic or a plumber, anything but a literary lawyer and cultural commentator, as I used to be introduced on television. I did not even look particularly Indian. All that was clear was that I belonged to that difficult category, the immigrant.

The day after my arrival in Montreal, I rented a modest apartment with parquet floors in an older red-brick building in a mainly English-speaking neighbourhood. Then, as I had done prior to my move to the village, I went to the public library. I soon found what I was looking for: an island chain called the Turks and Caicos. It had a population of 30,000 people, two per cent of whom identified themselves as East Indian. Two percent of 30,000 was six hundred people. The odds of running into one of them in Montreal were negligible.

Frazzled by my ordeals, I spent five days sleeping and setting up my apartment. Then I booked a sorely needed holiday. I flew to the Turks and Caicos. I stayed for two weeks, hired a car to drive around the main island, chatted with East Indian merchants in their ramshackle shops, attended a Sunday sermon in a stone church built by English colonialists, read up on the islands' history, and imagined where my ancestors might have lived if I had come from this place. I returned to Montreal confident in my identity as Ric Singh, who had immigrated to Canada from the Turks and Caicos as a teenager, then lived in Toronto for many years before moving to Montreal.

Here in the materialistic West, I found, I was able to engage in *punarjanma*, or reincarnation, without the inconvenience of relinquishing my body. I shook off the claims of India, of Hindus and Sikhs; my religious upbringing, if anyone asked about it, was West Indian Methodist. I felt relieved, but also anxious. At the first literary event I attended, I was cornered by a garrulous Bengali, who obliged me to lapse into taciturn grunts to keep my shadow Indianness under wraps. The most pressing danger, I grasped, was not that a West Indian would realize I was not like him but that an East Indian would realize I was. Fortunately, in this regard, Montreal was not Toronto; far fewer of my compatriots had settled here than in southern Ontario. I had chosen the right city in which to hide out from Indianness.

I devoted my days to compiling a plausible CV, elaborating my work of art as though it were a sculpture of which Ric Singh was the result. Pangs of furious regret ripped through me as I realized I would never again enjoy a lawyer's respect or financial security. I spent hours mulling over the possibility of a phone call to the Law Society of Upper Canada to ask about the procedure for reinstatement to the Ontario Bar. Yet I knew it was hopeless; and if I phoned Toronto legal institutions from a Montreal number, I was in danger of exposing myself: a single leak to the newspapers and my self-reinvention would have to start again in Texas. Fraternization with my past was off limits. The only heritage I could carry with me, because it enriched me without marking me, was my reading. My imagination would always be animated by the lessons of the Victorians; in the depths of my soul I would remain an aspiring squire.

With this in mind, I constructed my CV from the rubble of the life I had lost, inserting references to work on community newspapers, columns written for small publications, fictitious book reviews and minor feature articles that no one would be able to trace. I gave myself a B.A. in English literature from Lakehead and an M.A. from Western. I bought the Montreal *Gazette* and picked up the free arts tabloids to learn about local reference points, local outlooks on Canada and the world. Whenever I spotted a promising literary event, I went to it. My fears of running into someone I had known in Toronto were appeased by the realization that literary life in Montreal had few points of contact with the glamorous pageant

I had feasted on as a southwestern Ontario lawyer. I asked people I met at these events about
their day jobs. Some taught in Quebec's system
of junior colleges, others translated business materials between English and French, many scraped
by on irregular teaching or editing contracts. At
a particularly uninspired poetry reading, I made
polite conversation with a friend of the hapless
poet. Miguel was dark, with a long, woebegone
face that belied the burliness of his robust chest
and shoulders. He did not reveal where he had
been born, but mentioned that he had travelled
in the Caribbean. He invited me out for a beer.
(Ric, unlike R. U., drank beer. I savoured Molson
Canadian and Labatt Blue. I learned how to pro-
nounce Belle Gueule, and how to order one in
French.) In between telling me about his adventures in Trinidad, my new companion mentioned
that a friend worked for one of the free newspapers that was hurled into driveways in districts
where people lived in houses rather than apartments. "You should send him a CV," he said. "I
think he'd like you."

His hand lingered on my shoulder, then
dropped to my hip. I excused myself to go to the
toilet. The warmth of Miguel's palm in a place

where men's palms did not usually rest made me less uncomfortable than I would have expected. Since having myself shorn in Kingston, I had felt pared to a male essence that gravitated to the company of men. The lust that had driven me into Chyou's bed and body in search of the vital counterpart to the other, more ethereal woman in my life, fell into abeyance. I ceased to sleep with women. I did not sleep with men, either, but I craved their camaraderie, their bulkiness, their muscularity, their solidity, their ineptitude at deception. I did not care whether the men I talked and drank beer with slept with women or men or, as was sometimes the case, with both. Uncaring of their orientation, I revelled in male directness and male simplicity. The cultural maze of my life had grown too intricate: I longed for straight talk and company detached from concealed strings. Or, if I did not, Ric did. Being Ric was less disorienting than being the southwestern Ontario lawyer: I experienced the impression Ric made on others only from the inside; I did not see him on television or read about what he said in the newspapers. Talking to men anchored me in my new persona in a straightforward way. When I returned from the toilet, Miguel gave me a smile and touched my hip. "I'm going to tell my friend he should interview you."

He was as good as his word. I called the number he gave me and was invited to drop off a CV, then come around two days later for an interview. I answered my new employer's questions in a manly monotone. After my holiday in the Turks and Caicos, I had affected a West Indian lilt. I squelched this caprice when I discovered that being an obvious West Indian invited prejudices even more virulent than those endured by East Indians. An East Indian might be a Paki, but a West Indian was a ganja-monger, a hood, a man who was feared as being both lazy and violent. I spoke in ambiguous tones, revealing my Turks and Caicos origins to new acquaintances by cautious stages that allowed them to interject, "But you've been here for a long time," or, "You're Canadian now."

During my interview, I emphasized my Canadian university education, my itinerant career on community newspapers. I got the job. It did not pay well, but I earned enough to live on. I was able to stop depleting my handsome send-off. Located on an upper floor of an aging industrial building on the edge of Old Montreal, the tabloid thrived on advertising. Four-fifths of the publication was publicity and supermarket coupons. The first three pages contained hard news, pulled off the wire, or rewritten by employees who had simply listened to the radio; local news stories, sports line scores, and announcements of cultural events were squeezed in around the advertising over the remaining eighty pages. The paper appeared once a week, on Thursday, and hit the driveways of Notre-Dame-de-Grâce, the Town of Mount Royal, Montreal West, Côte-Saint-Luc, Westmount and other anglo residential neighbourhoods, out to the West Island, on Friday morning. Having slotted me as an intellectual after I had answered a question about my hobbies by saying that I liked to read Victorian novels, the editor assigned me to compile the cultural listings. I learned about every jazz and rock concert, experimental theatre production, and poetry reading in the city.

I attended few of the events that I arranged into columns. I was now employed, inhabiting a bare-knuckle form of literary existence. My life having passed its mid-Victorian zenith of glory and abundance, I had declined into the nether world of *fin de siècle* disillusionment. In the evenings, riding the metro to work, I read less Dickens and Trollope, and more George Gissing. Surrounded by culture in French, I amused myself with the decadent prose of J. K. Huysmans and Remy de Gourmont. I was aware that I was scraping by in a premature autumn of life, an autumn that lacked any glimmer of the sweetness Chyou expected in hers. My boon days of television appearances, tuxedo dinners, famous acquaintances, and generous retainers from charitable boards could not return. Montreal, which had also passed its peak of glory, was the proper city in which to live this life. With its skyline held low by the brooding mountain, the neighbourhoods dispersed by the contorted geography of a city bunched around a solidified blob of magma, it was limping into the future on its cumulative inheritance from the past. If I could no longer be a squire, I wished, in spite of the burly exterior I now displayed, to be a man steeped in history. Montreal was drenched in the residue of the past; if I could no longer afford to be rural, then an urbanity that was stately and quasi-European suited me better than exile to pseudo-modern towers beyond the last subway station. In Montreal, in contrast to Toronto, immigrants did not have to settle in the outskirts;

old and new residents mingled in the city's core.

I told myself that if these days were depressing by comparison with those I had lived as a literary squire, they were far better than my years with my cousin. Then I had lost myself; now I had chosen to change who I was. Then I had been dependent, now I was independent. Then, celibacy had been imposed upon me ... And now? Now I was waiting for Ric to tell me who he was.

After work I wandered uphill out of Old Montreal until I reached René-Lévesque or Sainte-Catherine. I found my way to bars or clubs or a movie, or a café where I sat down and read. I had been in Montreal for less than a month when I walked past the mansion where I had spent my final joyful hours with Milly. It was boarded up. The club had closed and the old wooden house was falling into disrepair. It was gone, as my provisional beard was gone. I was no longer in drag; but who had my shaving exposed? I sat at bars on the eastern stretch of Sainte-Catherine, enjoying the closeness of other men's bodies. Thoughts of Milly clustered like a barricade, preventing me from moving on. Chyou had vanished like my beard: she had been my lover and it had ended; but with Milly nothing had ever started, and for that reason nothing could finish. If I had been able to complete her separation agreement, that document that had thwarted me, would we still be teasing each other today? Would I have survived disbarment, or avoided it, to loiter longer in the gardens of loiterature? Or would Milly's departure for Saskatchewan have drained away my protective moat, leaving me exposed and vulnerable to being dropped by television panels and charitable boards? The rumbling of these trains of thought through the tunnels of my mind carried me into a past I had abandoned, stymying my exploration of the life of Ric Singh.

In my second year working at the tabloid, it happened. A press release crossed my desk: not local poets this time, but a reading sponsored by a major publisher, featuring writers who were famous. I began to type it into the "Literary" column on my screen. My fingers slipped on the keys as I realized that the first name was that of the bearded swashbuckler. The second name rang a distant bell. I closed my eyes and remembered the girl from the Annapolis Valley who, like me, had done favours to people who mattered. My reading of the newspapers in recent years, and particularly of the book sections, had informed me that her career was on the rise. Now, I saw, she had the same publisher as the swashbuckler, and read with him on an equal billing. Her record of service was immaculate, her upward trajectory unstoppable. I clenched my fists for a second, then leaned forward, preparing to save the entry. Only then did I see that the two writers were being introduced by the president of the University of South Saskatchewan, Dr. Millicent Crowe.

I drew a tight breath. I typed Milly's name into the entry and saved it. One of our scribblers later wrote two paragraphs on the swashbuckler and the girl from the Annapolis Valley. The reading became one of our three "Top Picks in the Arts" for that week.

At the end of the work day, I went home to my flat. I did not want to leave my bedroom until Milly's visit to Montreal was over. If I saw her, tough Ric would disintegrate, shattering into the fragments of a disgraced southwestern Ontario lawyer. Yet if I let this opportunity pass, when again would I have the chance to talk to her? The only thought that perturbed me more than not being able to settle into my life as Ric was the prospect of being merely Ric forever, of never recovering my vanished glory, of not knowing what had really happened between us. I should ignore this literary event, as I ignored so many others. I would not be the man I was now if I allowed spirits from an earlier incarnation of my soul to agitate and disturb me. Yet my anxieties bore me away. They would not allow me not to take a peek at my Milly.

The event took place in a large conference room at the back of a five-star hotel. As I entered, glad of the darkness, I glanced at the long table and the brightly lit podium at the front. A voice hissed at me. My heart contracted: but it was not Milly, it was Miguel. I hesitated; tonight I wanted to be alone. Miguel stood up and waved. Seeing I had no choice, I sat down next to him. I thought of all that I could not explain to him; of how a certain R. U. Singh, attorney-at-law, did not belong with him but with the famous figures preparing to read and speak. Three years ago I would have been up there with them, my turban bobbing at the front of the room. Only the weight of Miguel's hand on my shoulder prevented Ric from dissolving into R. U.

A man who wore a garish purple tie got up to welcome us, recite a list of sponsors and remind us that books would be available for sale and signing.

He introduced Milly. She walked to the podium in a white pantsuit, her billowing blond hair throwing into relief a stiffness in her stride that had not been there before. With the fading of her feminine fluidity, her slacks now lent her a mannish air. Milly, like me, had been melted down to a male essence. If the young men in the club could see her now, they would imagine that it was she, not I, who was in drag.

"This lady is a big shot," Miguel whispered, leaning close to me. "They say she's going to be the next president of McGill."

"Good evening, ladies and gentlemen," Milly said, in her neutral, even, clearly articulated voice. It was her professional speaking voice, not the voice she used for private conversations; even so, it drove a spar of heat into my chest. "I'm going to start with a confession. I am a Fugitive. When I say that, people assume I am a political refugee— or a criminal." She paused for the laughter, then went on: "Fugitive, for me at least, has a different meaning. I grew up in the old American South, partaking of a literary culture dominated by the ghosts of a school of critics that included my illustrious relative John Crowe Ransom."

I was outraged. Milly had broken our pact.

She had drawn attention to the fact that she was not Canadian by birth, daring to place herself outside the circle within which she and I had danced. I groped to understand how, after the effort she had made to Canadianize her accent and antecedents, she could do such a thing. Was it the spirit of the post-Cold War era that freed her to embrace a heritage she used to renounce as a liability when it dripped from her husband's every drawled word and exaggerated gesture? Her confident tone—when had Milly been less than confident? When had she done anything without having calculated the consequences?—allowed me to see that being a university president had made her impervious to the opinions of others. Her position had bestowed on her the prerogative of ignoring what Canadians thought. She was above the fray, as the masters at the Academy used to say in admiration of people who were superior to their peers, ensconced in the high-salaried establishment (I wondered how much a university president earned), oblivious to petty griping or assertions that she did not belong. Her talk, an introduction to the two writers and an essay on the value of art and the Arts, was also an advertisement for her own prominence. I suspected that Miguel was right. Dr. Millicent Crowe had come to Montreal to audition for an important job. Among the audience in this crowded theatre were movers and shakers who were in attendance not to hear the writers, but the woman who was introducing them.

I stared at the stage with such intense concentration that I was oblivious to the warmth of Miguel's palm on my thigh. Milly finished her speech, and bowed to acknowledge a round of spirited applause. The readings passed in a blur. The swashbuckler read in his muted, remotely English accent. His eyes darted, half-squinting at the crowd, in the same expression he used to send in my direction when spinning tall tales of the Orient by the fountain, seeming to fear I would expose his exaggerations. The young woman from the Annapolis Valley shook her blond curls and read with a passion that folded into self-absorption of a strain that the crowd found charming. Then the man in the purple tie was back on stage, exhorting the crowd to buy the writers' books and have them signed. In an instant, huge queues had formed in front of both writers. Milly sat between them at the long table, smiling in satisfaction, as though each writer's success were her creation.

I got to my feet.

"Are you going to buy—?"

Ignoring Miguel, I walked to the front of the room and inserted myself between the twin lines of book buyers. I strolled towards the table. Ahead of me, bathed in the lights, I saw Milly smile, then respond to a comment made by the swashbuckler as he signed a book. The man in the purple tie came up behind her. She reached up and shook hands with him over her shoulder. She made a comment to the young woman writer, then laid a hand on her shoulder. Her head turned and she looked forward again, taking in the writers' twin lines of book-clutching admirers, the crowd that continued to mingle behind my back in the gloom. Her face was folded into a wide-mouthed smile whose familiarity drilled into me like no other facial expression on earth.

I walked towards her. I felt as though I were approaching the Queen to be knighted, or the Governor General to receive the Order of Canada.

No, not the Order of Canada.

I would ask Milly why.

I walked forward, step by step. Her smile dried up as she saw me coming. I glimpsed no warmth in her face, no recognition, only the wariness of the public figure managing the unruly crowd. Even though she was unfamiliar with my beardless face and turban-less crewcut crown, I felt certain that my gait, my carriage, would tell her instantly that her old, dear friend R. U. was paying her a visit.

I placed my hands on the table and looked down into her face. "I am also a fugitive," I said.

"A fugitive, at least in my sense, is not a refugee." She hadn't recognized me. She was on automatic pilot, responding as one did to half-witted comments from the punters by repeating basic tenets of one's talk. In doing this, she had given me my opening.

"You think that just because I am brown I must be a refugee! That is racism. I am as Canadian as you are—"

She looked terrified. "I'm sorry. I wasn't suggesting—" She glanced over her shoulder as though to check whether the man in the purple tie had overheard the exchange. "I would never say that. You've misunderstood. I was speaking of the critical movement in the U.S. South—"

"If you're from the South, you must be a racist." I could not resist pricking her with one more jibe. Then I laughed with all the gusto my chest could muster. Now, I thought, she would recognize me, in spite of my changed appearance. My laughter had been a constant feature of our friendship; along with the pattering of the rapids and her husband's drawl, it had been the soundtrack of her village life. "You must not let me get the better of you, Milly. You and I were fellow fugitives for so long." I stared down into her face. Her features had become motionless. "Come on, Milly. It's your old friend R. U. Don't you recognize me? Did you think I would disappear forever? This is Canada. Nobody goes away. Didn't you tell me that was a reason to be cautious in my dealings with people? Because here in Canada people always come back?"

"You're talking gibberish," she said, looking down at the table.

"'The United States and India are big enough for people to disappear into other lives. Canada is not.' Well, you were right. Here I am. Remember the last time we were together in Montreal? How we sat in that gay club and planned our futures?"

The young woman from Nova Scotia directed a worried look in my direction, then a questioning look at Milly. I addressed the young writer. "I was present, miss, when it was decided that you would become famous. We were all sitting at the oak table in Milly's back garden, the fountain was on, and Milly said—"

"You're delusional!" Milly looked up into my face. For a brittle moment, our eyes met: eyes that had gleamed together in complicity, both in private and under bright lights. Now, rather than inviting my companionship, they deflected my gaze. Milly glanced at the swashbuckler. He kept his head down and continued signing. He was more Canadian than she.

Milly's mouth tightened. I sensed that she had reached a decision as to how she would address me. "You're delusional, and I don't know who you are." She answered the young writer's interrogating glance: "This nutcase has the crazy idea that he knows me."

"Nutcase!" I said. "How dare you!? I am R. U. Singh, the southwestern Ontario lawyer. Your neighbour for many years, who did you favours just as this young woman did." I appealed to the young woman writer. "Have you heard, miss, of the southwestern Ontario lawyer R. U. Singh?"

"Ric!" Miguel's hand pawed at my sleeve. "What are you doing, man? You're gonna get into trouble."

Milly smiled. "Ric! You're suffering from delusions, Ric. You think you're someone else."

The ruckus had caught the attention of the man in the purple tie. He approached Milly from behind, waving to figures in the wings. Milly cocked her head as though addressing an auditorium, though I could see that her words were directed at the young writer, and at her host. "You're right that I had a friend named R. U. Singh. He ran into difficulties with his law career and moved back to India. You're not R. U. Singh!"

Her listeners looked assuaged. The man in the purple tie flicked a hand in my direction. Two tall young men in red blazers and black slacks broke through the queue of the swashbuckler's fans and slipped behind me. Each one seized me just above the elbow with a grip that burned my flesh. "*Monsieur*, you leave now!" In his Québécois accent, "leave" sounded like "live." *You live now*. Yes, I thought, I'm living, I'm still alive, however hard that bitch may try to kill me. I swore I would cease being Ric. I would return to Toronto, reassume my identity as R. U. Singh, disbarred southwestern Ontario lawyer, and denounce Milly. Yet even as they hauled me away, Miguel trailing in our wake like the embarrassed owner of an aggressive hound, I knew that no one in Toronto would heed me. The South Asian community groups, whose support I would need to take my case to the media, loathed me. Television and radio producers would flee from having me on their shows. It was hopeless. One never feels so hopeless as when one is being manhandled. As they hustled me back up the aisle between the two long lines of well-dressed people waiting to have their books signed, I shouted: "Why did you do it, Milly? Why did you complain about me to the Law Society? One day we were best friends and the next day you betrayed me!"

The young woman from the Annapolis Valley had stopped signing. Her eyes were fixed on me in consternation. Milly paid no attention either to her or me. She had stood up and was shaking her head as she chatted with the man in the purple tie. That was the last time I saw her in person.

A moment later I was out on the cold Montreal street. The bouncers waved their hands at me. "Stay away, *Monsieur*! Go home if you do not want more trouble." Then, one lowered his voice: "*Espèce de Tamoul!*"

I had been in Montreal long enough to know that the final words meant the bouncer had recognized me as East Indian, not West Indian. He was not being complimentary about this fact. Layers of my being crashed down on each other. I felt as vacant as the derelict club where Milly and I had communed for the last time. Before I knew what had happened, I had burst into tears.

"Ric," Miguel said, giving me a hug. "You lost it, man. You thought you were somebody else."

"I am somebody else."

"We're never who we think we are, huh?" He clapped my shoulder. "Come on, man. Let's go have a beer."

"It's too late for a beer," I sobbed. "If I have a beer now, I'll cry all night."

He smiled. "Come to my place. I'll stop your crying."

FIFTEEN
jude the obscure

I saw no shadow of another parting from her.

My rage roared on for days after my ejection from the hotel. I asked my boss if I could write an article for the tabloid. He gave me cautious assent, yet I was too angry and confused to put words on paper. All of my credentials, my degrees, the professional status I had flaunted, had melted away. There were no more B.A.s or M.A.s to summarize my life, merely the private designation *Fugitive (failed)*. I had failed to become what Milly was. Yet, starting on the night of that last encounter, I began to become someone else. Late that night, as Miguel inhabited me, I inhabited Ric as I never had before. I became the person I had chosen to be. The sting of Milly's dismissal lingered for weeks, delaying my sloughing-off of the final leavings of the southwestern Ontario lawyer. Yet, as one skin peeled away, another grew. I continued to read gloomy *fin de siècle* fiction: Gissing; late, pessimistic Thomas Hardy; the socialist novels of Jack London. My days of Kim, burned by the Indian sun, meeting the woman in white, were over. But, though I was obscure, I did not suffer the fate of Jude. My mind caught the glimmer of possibilities, the bright lights of the twentieth century peeping over the horizon of the literature I read as my body cavorted towards the twenty-first century in a brotherly wrestling with Miguel. I realized that like the southwestern Ontario lawyer R. U. Singh, the Montreal journalist Ric Singh could have a career on his own terms. Indeed, Ric would be less dependent on others' approval than R. U. had been. My loitering in literary gardens had given me a range of reference possessed by no one else in my office. Two years after joining the tabloid, I was promoted to deputy editor. From this position I would be able to jump to another publication, then another, until I was writing real journalism.

I could not suppress all of my memories. I accepted that it would be unhealthy to do so. So, one day, I allowed a niggle of curiosity to become a quiver of action. In a momentary lull in the daily rush, I looked up the number of our sister tabloid in Saskatchewan. We shared content with other papers in the chain; now and then it fell to me to speak to editors elsewhere in the country. "Hello," I said, with newshound gruffness. "This is Ric in Montreal. I'm fact-checking a story on the houses of university presidents across the country. What can you tell me about the residence of the president of the University of South Saskatchewan?"

"I can tell you where it is," my Western counterpart replied. "It's been in the same house for decades. Now that you mention it, there's been a pile of work out there recently. The new prez is some big shot from the East. She's having the place renovated."

"Can you tell me whether she's having a fountain built in the back garden?"

"A fountain? Are you serious?"

"It's a detail I'm trying to verify." I heard a catch in my voice.

"A fountain on the prairies! That would be a new one. I can't say. Maybe I should send somebody out to take a look at the renovations. There could be a story there. Do you want me to get back to you about the fountain?"

"No," I said. A chill had settled between my shoulder blades. "I'll cut that part."

I had lapses such as these, yet I grew more confident in my life. I was no longer the passive fellow who had sat in his flat above the rapids and waited for others to do him favours. I told the left-armed fast bowler that I had decided to pursue the journalistic, rather than the legal, thread of my career, and that it had led me to Montreal. I gave him to believe that my passion for the bodies of white women coursed on unabated. If I wished to receive a share of my father's estate—the reduced share of a fifth son—I could not allow the fast bowler to suspect that the aspersions cast on me at the Academy had borne fruit on another continent. He must not know that I spent my evenings on the eastern stretch of Sainte-Catherine and my nights in the arms not of white women, but of a man who was nearly as brown as we were. I could not reveal that I went out to brunch on Sundays with groups of men who exchanged gossip about the lives and feelings of other men. I shared with my eldest brother the news that I had discovered an island chain in the Caribbean where I took a holiday every year. I did not tell him that the purpose of my visits was to consolidate the masquerade that I had been born in that place.

The tabloid's editor left, lured away by a corporate in-house magazine. I took over his job on an interim basis. Management put me on probation. Three months from now I might be confirmed as editor; even if I wasn't, the experience would stand me in good stead. The paper's layout and organization was my responsibility. I tilted the coverage more towards the arts and international news. I decided which stories ran, and on which pages. One day the new deputy editor sent me a story from Canadian Press. "It's too crazy to run," he said, coming over to my desk, "but you might get a laugh out of it."

I looked at my screen and froze. A photograph of Milly appeared: Milly hunched and glowering, her pale suit accentuating the sickly pallor of her face, as she was escorted out of a boardroom by men in suits who gripped her arms as securely as the bouncers had seized mine.

The President of the University of South Saskatchewan has been dismissed for misappropriation of

202

funds. Dr. Millicent Crowe was removed from a meeting of the university's board of governors on Monday after a local newspaper revealed that she had drawn on an internal budget to refurbish the president's official residence. Among the extravagances attributed to Dr. Crowe was the importation of marble from Carrara, Italy to construct a fountain in the backyard ... Dr. Crowe, an American, was said to have alienated senior administration and the board of governors with her aggressive style.

Fugitive (Failed).

"You see that?" the deputy editor said. "An Italian fountain in Saskatchewan! What a laugh."

I closed my eyes, imagining long afternoon conversations with good wine and illustrious company. I could do Milly a favour, in my small way, by burying this story.

"Maybe on the back page?" my deputy said. "Just for kicks? Or do you want to forget about it?"

"No," I said, "if it bleeds it leads. I want that photograph at the top of the front page, and the story right below it."

He looked startled.

"You heard what I said. This woman almost became president of McGill. The end of her career is big news."

Later, consumers of mainstream media would learn that Montreal journalist Ric Singh had helped to break this story. In doing so, as I alone knew, he had relinquished his allegiance to fugitives. I went back to work, untroubled by any life prior to my present.

ACKNOWLEDGEMENTS

I thank Linda Leith for giving Mr. Singh a home and Katia Grubisic for editing the manuscript with just the right ear. I'm grateful to my stepfather, Robin MacDonald, for his extensive comments on an early draft of this novel, as well as for several decades of conversation about Victorian novels.

ALSO BY STEPHEN HENIGHAN

NOVELS
Other Americas
The Places Where Names Vanish
The Streets of Winter
The Path of the Jaguar

SHORT STORY COLLECTIONS
Nights in the Yungas
North of Tourism
A Grave in the Air

NON-FICTION
Assuming the Light: The Parisian Literary
    Apprenticeship of Miguel Ángel Asturias
When Words Deny the World: The Reshaping
    of Canadian Writing
Lost Province: Adventures in a Moldovan
    Family
A Report on the Afterlife of Culture
A Green Reef: The Impact of Climate Change
Sandino's Nation: Ernesto Cardenal and Sergio
    Ramírez Writing Nicaragua, 1940-2012.

Printed by Gauvin Press
Gatineau, Québec